UMBRELLA

— A PACIFIC TALE —

Ferdinand Mount

Minerva

A Minerva Paperback
UMBRELLA

First published in Great Britain 1994
by William Heinemann Ltd
This Minerva edition published 1995
by Mandarin Paperbacks
an imprint of Reed International Books Ltd
Michelin House, 81 Fulham Road, London SW3 6RB
and Auckland, Melbourne, Singapore and Toronto

A CIP catalogue record for this title
is available from the British Library
ISBN 0 7493 9543 5

Printed and bound in Great Britain
by Cox & Wyman Ltd, Reading, Berkshire

Any resemblance to – well, most
of the history in this story
is truer than most history,
but all the characters in it are dead,
millions of them, so they cannot be libelled,
though they could be mourned.

— I —

Thought had gone into the purchase, a good deal of thought. He had been thinking of it from the moment he had wished the lodge porter good morning and walked through the gates down Oxford Street. Stout it had to be. That was the inescapable word. A flimsy parasol would not even keep out the thin rain now spotting the shoulders of his greatcoat. For the north of Scotland only the robustest of umbrellas would do. He could still remember from his childhood the driving easterly storms, the great bucketfuls of water streaming down inside his collar, the sludge underfoot, his Gordon tweed cape turned to porridge. Walking through the sweet shabby fringes of Soho – the little snuff shop in Swallow Street, the idlers already sheltering under the arcade – he remembered above all how cold he had been, colder indoors than out, the noise of his wet boots squelching on the marble pavement of the great hall – its frigid elegance his first encounter with the classical, Mr William Adam's finest piece of work. And his grandfather – no grander nobleman in all Scotland, so grand he always referred to himself with scant command of grammar as 'Us' – bellowing 'boots, boy, boots'. His mother hated paying these duty calls at Haddo. Well, she hated Us, with his mistresses and his illegitimate children scattered around the country as though six legitimate children and four castles were not enough to satisfy his appetite for possessions (the domain of Us stretched from the Atlantic to the German Sea, it took three days' hard riding to cross the desolate expanse of it).

He found his eyes watering at the thought of his mother. The boy had weak lacrimal ducts, the Edinburgh doctor opined, when he had called to see his mother when she was dying and Us asked if he could find out why the boy never stopped snivelling, hadn't stopped snivelling in fact since his father had been thrown by a horse (the horse had been startled by the sudden clanking of a bucket as the maid drew water from a well in the courtyard) and died four years earlier. Orphaned. There was something to be said for orphaning. It stiffened the will, hardened whatever iron nature had put into you. At the age of fourteen he had chosen his own guardians (or curators, as they called them in Scotland), Mr Pitt and Mr Dundas – the most powerful men in the two kingdoms, had sent himself to Harrow School in defiance of Us (who refused to foot the bills until shamed into it by Mr Dundas), had shut his ears to the beastliness and the bullying at that rough academy, had virtually given himself a classical education, and now Us was dead and he was going north to claim his inheritance. And he needed an umbrella.

With a jump he saw that he was already outside Brigg's shopfront and there was Brigg himself, peering out through the steamy panes and the array of walking sticks and umbrellas like a Newgate prisoner peering through the bars. Brigg swung the door open before his own hand had touched the handle.

'Good morning, sir, good morning. A fine morning for us if not for you.' Brigg was as dry and spare as the ribs of his umbrellas, not a drop of water could ever have fallen on his withered brow or slid down his pomaded scalp.

'I have come to purchase an umbrella.'

'You have come to the right place, sir. I have the most elegant article in town, waterproofed silk of the finest quality, steel ribs and a slender beechwood handle with brass fittings and a twenty-four-carat gold band. There.' With a brisk darting motion of one hand, he swung the slender umbrella into the air and then with the other he opened it. There was a sharp thwang as the ribs clicked into place. The taut arcs of jet black silk, the rich chestnut sheen of the handle, the flash of gold just below its curve, like a wedding ring sealing the umbrella's ownership – the elegance of the article could not be denied.

'That is a first-class umbrella, but I am afraid I need something a little stouter.'

'Stouter?' Brigg paused, uncertain how to phrase a respectful objection.

'Stouter.'

'Most gentlemen seem to prefer a more slender design.'

'In that case, I am not most gentlemen.'

'Are you perhaps looking for something more in the nature of a coachman's umbrella?'

'Perhaps I am.'

'I sold one of these to young Lord Byron last week. He seemed very satisfied with it. Just up from Harrow School he was, a fine young gentleman.'

'Ah yes. He is my cousin, as it happens.'

And so he was, and a resentful, teasing, arrogant little brat of one too – resentful particularly, for did not their names start off the same 'George Gordon', before Byron's dwindled into a mere barony and an encumbered estate somewhere in the Midlands while his – but he was determined not to succumb to the arrogance of great possessions which had ruined the happiness of both their families (Byron's father Mad Jack had gambled away the Castle of Gight which his wife had brought him, otherwise their lands would have marched).

'Well then, perhaps your lordship too . . .'

He swung the heavy black umbrella gently to and fro and then handed it back to Mr Brigg.

'That is certainly stout enough, but it seems somewhat funereal. Do you have something a little more . . . rustic?'

'I have the very thing. I like to call it the Fisherman's Friend. Several anglers of my acquaintance have been good enough to tell me that it has transformed their piscatorial excursions.' From under the counter Mr Brigg drew out an umbrella of even larger size and more solid construction, but this time the material was of deep apple green, the sombre green of unripe cooking apples. Lord Aberdeen balanced it on the palms of his hands, feeling the weight of it.

'If your lordship would care to open it . . .'

'I was brought up to believe that it brought ill fortune to open up an umbrella indoors.'

'This is privileged ground, sir. Providence has granted us what you might call a professional dispensation.'

Mr Brigg took back the umbrella and pushed down its thick metal ring. The ribs were stiff and they settled into place with a heavier thunk than the town umbrella. The brass fittings were as thick as plumbers' accessories. The span of the umbrella was magnificent. Standing side by side under it, the two men were bathed in a warm green light.

'You could feed a whole family under this one, sir,

and all stay dry as a bone the livelong day.'

They smiled at one another. Mr Brigg had a shy attractive smile which shone unexpectedly out of his face. About his own smile, there was something awkward, he was not quite sure what. Even as a child, he had unnerved people when he smiled. Don't grin at me like a monkey, boy, Us used to bellow. And staring at the reflection of the two of them in Brigg's long glass, perhaps he did have a somewhat monkeyish aspect, with his square mask of a face and his bright Scottish button eyes.

'I'll have it,' he said, surprising himself by the roughness of his voice.

'Will your lordship send for it, or shall I have my boy deliver?'

'I shall take it with me. The rain is coming on heavy now.'

'It is a country umbrella, you know, sir. I should not like . . .'

'Don't take on, Mr Brigg. I shall not reveal where I obtained it to a living soul.'

He walked out into the grey morning and put up his great green umbrella. But the rain was beginning to soften again and the massy bulk of Burlington House reared out of it. Where had all the lightness of Wren and Gibbs gone to? He tilted the umbrella back to inspect the upper storeys and the cornice.

From nowhere a great splash of water wetted him from chest to toe. A chocolate-coloured curricle screeched and bounced to an untidy halt, the hooves of the two flashy bays slithering on the wet cobbles. A huge pink face surrounded by damp ginger whiskers leant out of the curricle.

'Hulloa, Haddock, off to sell oranges?'

'Ah Cupid. No, I'm off to hear my grandfather's will read.'

'Ye look like an orange woman with that contraption over your head.' Cupid was relentless. Like most persons with no sense of humour, he could never let go of a bad joke.

'Well, you look like Boadicea.' And indeed with his fleshy pink face and pouting mouth and frizzy ginger whiskers Cupid Temple did closely resemble the Queen of the Iceni as portrayed in a child's history book. He was always charging at people waving things – a cricket bat, pillows in the dormitory. He had half suffocated him with a pillow once, but then Aberdeen (Haddo as he still was) had got his revenge, taken him by surprise and locked him in the boot cupboard without a candle, shouting 'time for a little con-templation' – the sort of silly pun Cupid himself delighted in. But then Cupid recovered ground by chanting in his just-broken voice, 'Lighten our darkness, we beseech thee, O Lord', and Aberdeen let him out and they gave each other a hearty punch in the chest and pretended to be friends.

'I imagine that in Caledonia stern and wild you will be monarch of all you survey. Haddock of the North, now there's a title for you – rather you than me. In my opinion, barbarians begin north of Chatsworth.'

'Mr Hume and Mr Adam Smith would, I am sure, be most obliged to you for your opinion.'

'And the *women*, Haddock, not a sound tooth between 'em and all reeking of turnip and herring.'

How stiff and irritable he felt in Cupid's company, how impossible it was to explain the difference between true wit and this lame facetiousness, between genuine vivacity of conversation and this trumped-up bullfroggery.

'Well, I must not delay. M'lady of Seven Dials is waiting for me in her boudoir, and I must do her full justice before I dine with my father in Threadneedle Street.'

Aberdeen watched him rattle off down Piccadilly and shuddered. Everything Cupid said was not only inexpressibly vulgar but also curiously unconvincing, like an ill-cast actor playing a cad on the stage. Still, this rough chaff had left its mark. He could not deny a dread creeping up on him at the prospect of returning to Haddo. True, Us would no longer be there. That appalling, violent, sensuous vigour would no longer haunt the damp passages of the *piano nobile*. But what would Us have left behind? It was twelve years since he had come south and normal family life had ceased there.

All through the long journey north, he was conscious of leaving civilisation behind. There was .

grass in the streets at Edinburgh and an open sewer choked with excrement outside his lodgings. At Perth, the keeper of the rickety inn on the bridge (the George being full) could offer nothing to eat but sour beer and a dish of turnips. At Forfar, it was turnips again and mutton which would have served better as shoe leather. The horses were lame starveling hacks, the roads hard to distinguish from the desolate bog. There was no shelter against the lashing rain which stabbed at him from the ground upwards. Not a tree taller than a table, as Dr Johnson had said, and on the moors not a tree at all. North of Perth his bowels, always the most delicate of his organs, began to betray him. A griping pain was swiftly followed by uncontrollable spasms of diarrhoea. He crouched in the ditch with his nose brushing the dripping heather, while Tom the groom stood watch on the road above.

But even this odyssey had not prepared him for his first sight of Haddo. In fact, at the grimmest moments of the journey – the cloudburst outside Forfar, for example – he had begun quite involuntarily to summon up pleasant childhood memories of playing on the steps of Haddo with his sister Alicia, while Us, in a good mood (not as rare as all that, it had to be admitted), prodded them with his old shepherd's crook as though they were lambs at gambol. He remembered too how they crammed their mouths with blaeberries on the gentle slopes of Formartine and rolled over and over down the bouncy heather and then lay still at the bottom and listened to the buzzing of the bees.

It was only as they came up the long road from the south that he realised how selective his memory had been. For half a mile after passing through the lodge gates, they rode through a dismal swamp, a silent, mournful morass made more mournful still by the mew of a snipe zigzagging between the tufts of rushes. Then a broken-down fence and they were there. The big dull house squatted like a toad on the featureless plain, dead and shuttered. The windows on the ground floor were hidden by stacks of timber under makeshift sheds battened to the façade. No wonder there was scarcely a tree left standing for miles around. And they seemed to be running out of wood too. Under the lean-to sheds to the right he saw squares of fresh-cut peat in dripping piles up to the level of the windows of the great saloon. To his untutored eye, it looked highly improbable that these turves would ever dry out, certainly not unless the local tradition of horizontal rain underwent some divine interruption. Around the stacks of wood, two mangy brindled dogs were snuffling after rats.

The great door at the top of the steps opened and almost instantly was blown shut again, but not before Mr Crombie, the man of business, had slipped through it to greet the heir with the nearest approach to effusiveness permitted in Aberdeenshire.

'Ye'll have had a long journey,' he said in that put-upon, asking voice which George remembered as though it had been yesterday he had last heard it. 'And the weather's no been too douce either,' Mr Crombie added, with that dour understatement which went all too well with the voice.

Mr Crombie tugged the heavy door open, and they managed to step inside before the wind slammed it shut again. Half-a-dozen servants were standing shivering. The mould was so thick in the air you could smell it, although when George – we may presume on our intimacy in the heather to advance to Christian names, for when you have seen an earl at stool he never seems quite so much of an earl again (although we must not forget that all but half-a-dozen persons on the planet never called him anything except Lord Haddo or Lord Aberdeen) – when George advanced to greet them, the smell of their sweaty bodies was so strong and sour that the mould seemed fragrant by comparison. And as they opened their mouths to smile at him, nervously but warmly (for he was the first living hope that had come to their glum halls for years), he could not but notice that once again Cupid had been right. Even the two little housemaids with their black bootbutton eyes like his own had lost three or four teeth each, and Mrs Gordon the housekeeper – 'Ye'll have to get used to the sound of that name in these parts, your Lordship' – had only two yellow tombstones knocking against each other. Diet, that was the first thing that would have to be attended to – he made one of his mental notes. His mind had always been methodical and his bent serious, he had been the same at twelve as he was at eighteen and would be at thirty. Even his notes on Greek and Roman architecture were drawn up as smartly as a sergeant-major dressing his recruits.

And not just for the servants either, he further minuted to himself as Mrs Gordon brought a dish of turnips and leathery mutton to the cold, dusty little morning-room you could scarcely see out of because of the sodden timber piled high against the windows outside.

'The butler's sick, my lord,' she said, 'so I took the liberty.'

'I'm sorry to hear that, Mrs Gordon. I hope I may have the pleasure of meeting him as soon as he's recovered.'

'Och well, I doubt ye may have that privilege. He's mortal sick. The minister's been sent for. I hope the neeps'll be to your taste, sir. They're true Aberdeen-shire neeps.'

The small raw greenish mauve objects certainly had a taste of their own, a soursweet almost animal tang to them. George thought they would take some getting used to.

'She seemed reluctant to discuss the medical condition of the butler,' he observed to Mr Crombie who was sitting opposite him sipping a glass of rainwater madeira (he had declined the neeps, claiming to have recently breakfasted).

'It is a delicate matter.'

'Oh, you mean . . .'

'Mr Gordon is no flincher from the glass. An apoplexy has been diagnosed.'

'And the cellar?'

'Much depleted, I fear, my lord. I made an inspection in preparation for your arrival.'

'Well, no use crying over spilt milk. I suppose we had better proceed to the reading of the will.'

'Here, my lord? You would not prefer that we waited until you are recovered from the journey?'

'No, no, let us get on with it.'

And so he continued to chew at the mutton and gnash at the neeps – partly to annoy Mr Crombie, to whom he had taken a dislike – while the provisions of Us's will were read out in Mr Crombie's interrogative whine which sounded as though he could hardly believe what he was reading, although it was he together with the Writer to the Signet in Charlotte Square who had drawn up every last sub-clause in response to the instructions given by the Third Earl sitting bolt upright in bed in his dirty white nightshirt in the bedroom directly above where they were now sitting.

'Three thousand for Miss Susan, five thousand each for Mr Alexander, Mr Charles and Mr John. Your lordship may consider these provisions a trifle lavish for persons who have no legitimate claim upon the estate, since they have already been furnished with estates in the vicinity, but –'

'Proceed, Mr Crombie, proceed. I understand that all his lordship's children had to be provided for.' He masked his annoyance at being taken for a selfish miser by stabbing fiercely at the last neep, a particularly green one, and sending it skidding across the plate towards the Gordon arms on the rim – the boars' heads tongued and armed with the motto *fortuna sequatur*, advice which rang a little hollow at the present moment. In his case, Fortune seemed to be an elusive dame, judging by the provisions so far read out.

'A proper distinction is made between his late lordship's legitimate children and his other offspring.'

'You need not defend the provisions, Mr Crombie. I see nothing to criticise so far. Proceed.' In truth, his reserves of charity were being stretched, but he was damned if he was going to let Crombie see it.

They came to the end of the reading. George had not grasped all of it, but he had grasped enough. The legacies to his natural uncles and aunts and cousins were large, but they were not unfair. As for himself, he would not be able to live on the scale Us had lived (no human being ought to live on that scale), but he was not poor and the estate was not straitened. He thanked Mr Crombie for all the trouble he had taken.

'Ye'll wish to reflect and ponder, no doubt.'

'I shall.'

'If ye were thinking of maybe challenging some portions, I should counsel a mature period of reflection.'

'I have no such thoughts in my head.'

'Ah.' Mr Crombie had appeared to be standing on tiptoe almost, as he refilled George's glass. Now he subsided into his grey woollen stockings, and his grey pigeonbreast waistcoat gently deflated. 'Ye've a wise head on ye, your lordship, if I may venture to say so.'

'I am flattered, Mr Crombie. Would it be possible to take a breath of air, do you think?'

'Now?' Mr Crombie seemed startled.

'I cannot wait to see the old demesne.'

Mr Crombie looked out through the dirty windows. Even through the grime, it was possible to see above the logs that the sky was still full of rain.

'As your lordship pleases. I should be delighted to accompany you.'

'There will be no need for that.'

'I must insist. The ground is soft. And the short cut to the home farm is not well marked.'

That was no less than the truth. They seemed to be dodging from tuft to tuft in the bog. A pair of wild duck started a few yards ahead of them, quacking protest at this invasion of their wilderness. The rain blew harder into them so that George had to hold the umbrella in front of him like an ancient shield.

Peering to one side of the umbrella, he saw a field which had been roughly fenced and some rude efforts made at cultivation, although it was difficult to see whether the damp stalks were leftovers from some crop or merely weeds. At the far end of the field, at the limit of his vision, he saw a low brown shape moving with painful slowness along the hedge. At the end of the hedge the brown shape appeared to turn round and retrace its path at the same pace. He stopped, mesmerised by the gloomy passage to and fro of this thing. Mr Crombie, who had been walking a few paces ahead of him, to show the way, turned round to discover that he was now a hundred yards ahead and hurried back to his master.

'Is your lordship all right, is anything amiss?'

'What,' said George, pointing, 'what is that?'

'That,' said Mr Crombie, 'is Mrs Gordon.'

'Mrs Gordon?'

'Not the Mrs Gordon who is your lordship's housekeeper – if you are minded to keep her on, that is – no that is Mrs Helen Gordon of Tarves.'

And, indeed, as his eyes focused better, George could see that part of the brown shape was a woman bent forward, straining to pull a large object behind her.

'She has her own plough now,' Mr Crombie said.

'You mean, she is drawing the plough?'

'It is the custom in these parts. Our Aberdeenshire women are not afeared of hard work.'

'Oh,' George said. 'She is one of my tenants, I suppose.'

Mr Crombie laughed. 'Ye would have to walk many a mile in this direction to be quit of your lordship's land. Would you like to pass the time of day with her?'

'Perhaps it would be better not to interrupt her. She seems occupied.'

George walked on in silence. The path joined a harder broader road, and through the heavy mist he could make out a cluster of miserable thatched cabins, with the dark-brown sodden thatch of heather and rushes turning to a fearful green in patches. Beside each cottage the steam of the manure heap went up to be lost in the mist.

'This is Methlick village,' Mr Crombie said. Two children with bare feet came scampering down the road, splashing in the puddles. When they saw the factor and his master, they stopped and broke into laughter and began pointing.

'I didn't know we cut such a comic figure,' George said. Mr Crombie advanced, making angry gestures at the cheeky couple who went on guffawing and pointing. He broke into a run at them. They ran off a good deal faster and disappeared into one of the cottages, reappearing almost instantly, this time accompanied by an old man with a white beard and a scrawny woman in a pinafore who also broke into guffaws as soon as they saw Lord Aberdeen.

'Come, come, what is it?' George said.

'I can only suppose that they aren't used to strangers – no, no, it's your lordship's umbrella, that's what it must be.'

'My umbrella?'

Without thinking much about it, he reached up to

the heavy brass ring and drew the umbrella shut – at which the small crowd, now augmented by a tiny freckled boy no taller than a terrier, chattered and pointed with renewed enthusiasm.

'Haven't they seen an umbrella before?'

'It seems not, your lordship. I think they would be gratified if you would be kind enough to open it for them.'

'Would they just? Well, I'm not a performing bear.' But as the rain was coming down harder again, he did open it, with an ill grace, and the crowd clapped and laughed. The old man with the beard stepped forward and bowed politely; would his lordship close it just once more. George irritably shut the umbrella again and then opened it a third time because he was really quite wet now.

The old man exhaled a long, long sigh and shook his head. 'Eh, they're braw chiels i' the Sooth.'

That evening, George wrote letters to his friends, cheerful chaffing letters which made light of his situation. 'Alas this is not my Paradise: this is not Vall'ombrosa but a real Siberian waste. Far as the eye can reach no tree is seen. The desolation of the exterior is only equalled by the appalling badness of the house. As for the victuals, Mrs Gordon would be better employed as a cobbler than a cook. Tomorrow we are promised venison and I am already sharpening my axe.' In his sleep he dreamed of breaking the entail, disposing of the estate and taking ship for some warm southern climes, of exploring Delphi and Ephesus, of wandering through fields of anemone and asphodel and swimming at night in wine-dark seas under a velvet sky. But he slept only in short bursts, as the wind rattled the piles of timber outside the window and whistled through the lean-to sheds and then rattled the windows themselves. And as he shifted in the bed, the bedposts creaked, and the floortimbers creaked back, till once again he fancied he was at sea, heaving in an Aegean swell as the Dardanelles came into view and opened the way to a newer nobler world.

— II —

Should he go? He must go. The opportunity was golden. Peace at last and the whole Continent shimmering and open before him. Paris first, of course, or what was left of it, and then south, east, and south again. And when in Paris should he, could he – no, he must ask Mr Pitt first. After all, Mr Pitt had brought peace to Europe and might make his career. He did not want to upset his curator. The reply was prompt.

My dear Lord
   On my return from Cambridge yesterday evening I found your letter. If it were not for the circumstances you mention, I confess I should have rather inclined to doubt whether you would not have found it more advantageous to defer your visit to Paris to a later period; but I

certainly do not think that it is now desirable for
you to make any change in your plan.

The question of being introduced to Bonaparti
(if contrary to your expectation it should present
itself) seems to me to be one of mere etiquette,
and therefore to be best decided by whatever you
find practised by others in similar situations to
your own.

Believe me, my dear Lord,
Yours most sincerely
W. Pitt

There was undoubtedly a mild rebuke in those lines. It
was true he had not informed Mr Pitt until his plans
were well advanced, and as for Bonaparte – George
would now spell and pronounce the Consul's name *à
la française* – if he had not given assent, he had not
forbidden contact either. And to go to Paris without
paying a call on the enigma of his age, the monster, the
liberator, the tyrant, that would not be seeing Paris.

His luck was in. On a grey day on the Champ de
Mars, in front of that great honey-coloured Ecole
Militaire where Bonaparte had been a cadet, he had the
honour of being presented to the First Consul. He had
walked the length of the Champ de Mars with Mr
Jackson the English Minister, their umbrellas held aloft.
The immense silence was broken only by the faint hiss of
the rain on the sandy ground. The clunch-clunch of the
guards marching out through the arch of the Ecole
hardly provoked a sound from the crowds behind the
low wooden railing. They seemed unmoved even by the

first flip of the tricolors breaking above the lines of march. Perhaps, George thought, it was not done in France to show emotion at military parades. At home, by now they would have been cheering.

'Quick,' said Mr Jackson, 'if we hurry we might –'

Bonaparte had just dismounted from his white horse, and tossed the reins to an aide. He turned to meet the little group of dignitaries with an impatient irritable look about him. But when Mr Jackson, a little out of breath, stepped forward to introduce the young Lord Aberdeen, *le pupille de M. Pitt*, he stopped still on the damp tawny gravel and held out his hand with a warmth and alacrity that George was never to forget. He was a small man – that George had expected – and pale, sallow even, but slender and elegant, nothing puffed up about him, and with a wonderful brightness in his eye. An amused eye too, as George had some difficulty with the stiff ring on the umbrella and only managed to close it at the second attempt.

'Ah, two Englishmen with their umbrellas. That will surely bring us luck.' The aides tittered, the First Consul's smile became friendlier still, seemed to tell George to forget the titterers, to forget everything in the world but the two of them standing there on the wet gravel. George felt that the whole of France was gazing on him, such was the burning concentrated power of the Consul's eye. It was like the way at school they used to angle a magnifying glass to concentrate the sun's rays on a patch on one another's forearms in Long Meadow (Cupid always refused to stop until he had raised a red patch on one's skin).

'The ward of Monsieur Pitt. And how is dear Mr Pitt, we shall meet soon, very soon, I hope, to cement this peace with personal acquaintance, perhaps, who knows, even with friendship. I shall have to forget some of the things he has said about me, but then I know how to forget as well as how to remember.' His voice was croaky, a crow's caw. Even George could tell that it was a little stilted, the Rs too insistently rolled, the soft Gs a little too hard, a foreigner's voice, ugly perhaps to a French ear but somehow not unpleasing.

'Monsieur Pitt is very well. He sends his respectful regards' – although he had done no such thing, but the bare announcement of his curator's state of health seemed inadequate.

'You are dark, very dark for an Englishman. You could almost be a Frenchman.'

'I am a Scot.'

'A Scot, but how perfect. We shall revive the old alliance, together we shall bring England to her knees. What do you think of our review? You have noticed the detachments from the Helvetic and Batavian Republics and from Italy. They are fine men. When their regiments are all fully embodied, we shall have ninety thousand men on the frontiers of France, all ready to march at a moment's notice. What do you think of that, eh?'

'They look formidable.'

'They are formidable.' And as the First Consul went on to describe their organisation and training, George noticed again how quiet everyone was. The spectators were more numerous than ever, but they seemed somehow dulled. They might have been at a funeral. The First Consul's voice seemed to carry right across the vast misty parade ground, although he was nowhere near shouting. And George seemed to hear his own few stilted words of French rolling over the heads of the motionless troops. To his surprise, he found that he was losing the thread of the First Consul's remarks. Bonaparte's voice was fluid, urgent, enchanting, but he found some difficulty in attending to the sense of what he was saying.

'You will come and dine at Malmaison. The Citoyenne Bonaparte would adore to meet a dark Scotsman. And I should count it a privilege to entertain Mr Pitt's ward and hear more news of that great statesman.'

George bowed and stammered his thanks which were heartfelt, for such a visit was half his purpose in coming to Paris. At the same time, though, he began to be sensible of a certain delicacy in his position. He distinctly received the impression that the First Consul suspected there was more in George's visit than met that piercing eye of his. No doubt Mr Pitt would be eager to winkle out some hint of the First Consul's future plans, to form some estimate of the strength of his following in the country. Even if not explicitly dispatched as a spy, George could scarely help spying out something of the lie of the land. It would be futile to try to explain that in fact Mr Pitt had been dubious about George's coming at all and was unlikely to place any reliance on the word of an eighteen-year-old boy.

But these misgivings were swallowed up in a general nervous excitement as he rode up the little alley of limes on a mild afternoon of early spring and saw the pleasing seventeenth-century house, settled long and low on its gentle hillock overlooking a bend on the Seine. There was a harmless, casual look to the place. Even the rose garden, the pride of the Citoyenne Bonaparte, was an unpruned tangle at this time of the year. And the young cedar on the lawn, planted to celebrate the victory of Marengo, had a gawky air as though not expecting to stay long.

The First Consul was sitting in a low chair looking out of the window. He got up, came forward, and the afternoon light – the hazy heavy light of the Ile de France – caught his face and caught the smile on it, a smile of welcome but more than that, much more. The smile seemed to fill the room, irradiating the Sèvres porcelain on the *bonheur-de-jour* and the roses and faded cabbage greens of the tapestries. The world was suddenly full of hope, not a vague daydreaming sort of hope but a promise of action. And when the Citoyenne, as she still referred to herself not without a touch of mockery, came sweeping through the door behind him and tapped him on the shoulder to turn and be introduced, he felt he was being inducted into a conspiracy – no, that sounded mean – into an adventure.

Touching forty, she was still beautiful in her high-waisted white muslin gown with her beloved pink roses blowing in and out of its folds. By the standards of the ladies he had met in London, George supposed she might seem a little full-blown, blowsy even, but there was no resisting her even if he had wished to, which he did not because he wanted to adore her for her guillotined husband, for the roses on her gown and the warm touch of her hand on his shoulder.

'And so we have an English spy in our midst, how thrilling.' She made a little moue with her tiny mouth, giving George a glimpse of rotting yellow teeth.

'A Scottish visitor, madame.'

'Don't spoil my excitement. We live so quietly out here. You must not deny us our simple fantasies.'

'I will deny you nothing, madame.' How easy she made this banter. At home, he found light conversation the most arduous variety of intercourse.

'You hear that, Consul. A Scotsman who will deny me nothing. Does your Code cover that offence?'

'The Code deals most severely with all such offences. It will be one of the first Articles to be enforced when the Code becomes law.'

'If, Consul, if.'

'When, my dear. On the first of Germinal, you will see, it will be carried.'

'I am told, sir, that the opposition in the Legislative Body remains quite stubborn,' said George. Oh how stiff, how wooden – and into the bargain, how impertinent. But the smile on Bonaparte's face remained enchanting, unshadowed.

'Ah, my dear Lord Aberdeen, they are only pretending. They know that I am serious. They make splendid speeches promising to die for their rights, but when the time comes, we shall gallop up to their last ditch and look down and, pfft, it will be empty, and France will at last have a code of laws fit for a civilised modern country.'

The bay of the window looking out on to the garden, and on beyond down to the Seine, was on a higher level. Bonaparte stepped up on to this little platform – no more than seven or eight feet from end to end – and began to pace up and down it, dominating the long room with its low ceiling. George thought there was something theatrical about him, not in the sense of being false but of needing a larger audience. Besides, slight as he was, the dome of his noble forehead was nearly kissing the ceiling. The air was stifling. George began almost to hanker for the draughts which gusted through the little sitting-room at Haddo.

'In future, we shall not be able to afford such delays. We are an impatient people, my lord, and we are living through impatient times. You with your great estates, your ancestral contentment, cannot imagine the restless spirit that is sweeping through Europe. Why should you? If I had been brought up to look out of my castle windows knowing that everything within five leagues, I mean kilometres, belonged to me, then I would not be agitating for change. But as it is, my dear sir, look out of this window and what do you see, a pretty view, in summer a few roses –'

'More than a few, thousands of roses, in fact thousands and thousands,' Josephine, reclining on her uncomfortable-looking long chair (the sort made famous by Madame Récamier), protested with a lazy humorous pout of her amazingly small lips, like a child's mouth.

'– A few roses, but just beyond the river there are millions of people who do not enjoy your advantages, my lord.'

George wanted to protest to the effect that his considerable possessions had not so far brought quite the domestic tranquillity imputed to him but knew he could not enter so trivial an objection.

'They are without land, without money and many of them without hope. All they have is their nation and their liberty. Why should they not earn a certain immortality by extending those blessings to people who have neither?'

'Indeed,' George said.

'You say indeed in your reserved English way.'

'Scottish, my dear, he is Scottish,' Josephine drawled.

'Scottish, English, you are all Anglo-Saxons. You do not know, you cannot understand our passions. You cannot feel our impatience. I am thirty-three years old, I have been fighting battles since I was eighteen. I do not complain. That is my métier. It is the métier of our age. Do you know what they said in my report at the Ecole Militaire? "Will go far in favourable circumstances." Well, the circumstances are favourable. To fight, and to fight for liberty, that is the mission of our century. And our century must be led by people who know what it is to start from nothing, people who know how to cherish their liberty because they have nothing else to cherish.'

'But why then do some people speak of you as an enemy of liberty? Our newspapers, for example, complain that yours are controlled.'

'You spend too much time reading your newspapers, monsieur. You would be better occupied in visiting our magnificent new sewers. There you will find channels of communication which are clear and pure. *The Courier* is an abomination, but *The Sun* is worse, an utterly foul rag. Mr Pitt ought to have suppressed it.'

'But surely sir, the liberty of the press ought to be respected, with all its incidental evils.'

'Why, if the evils outweigh the good? Understand me, I don't hate liberty. Now and then it is necessary to move it out of the way when it is obstructing my route, the *route Napoléon*, but I understand liberty, I was nourished at its bosom.'

The room seemed unbearably hot now. And the little cups of strong coffee which were brought in made George's heart pulse uncomfortably quick. The Consul scarcely touched his coffee, set the cup down on a spindly little marquetry table and began pacing again. But now, sensing he had begun to provoke a kind of puzzled resentment in his listener, he turned to reminisce.

He talked of his campaigns in Egypt, how he had laid awake under the stars memorising the titles of all his corps and the names of the leading officers – and some of the old sweats in the ranks too – so that he could move among them on the morrow and rouse them to their destiny as comrades and intimates and join them to his vision of following in the footsteps of Caesar and Pompey. Egypt, he frankly confided, had only been the first step. He had pictured himself on the road to Asia, mounted on an elephant, with a turban on his head and a new Koran composed according to his own ideas. He would lead the mightiest army France had ever seen and attack the British power in India.

'It was a wonderful time, milord, the happiest time of my life. I was free to dream, and I am by nature fond of reverie. In the playground at Brienne, I used to sit in a corner and dream – until some other boys tried to turf me out of my corner, and then I would fight.' He switched on a glare of extreme ferocity and switched it off again instantly and smiled at George, exulting in the rapidity with which he could change his expression.

'But then I had to return to France. There was not a moment to lose, I mean that literally. In those affairs, thirty seconds too early or too late and pouf! But this was a time to be cautious. I lay low and let the Directory tremble, I let everyone tremble – tremble and hope. I knew that when the time came, their curiosity to see me would make them run after me. By the time I became First Consul, there was not a party in France which was not building its own hopes on me. Ah, the dinners I had to attend to receive the grateful thanks of this or that faction, the manufacturers of cannon and china, the notables of such and such a diocese, the returned émigrés, the lawyers, the stockbrokers – all imagining that I was their man, all needing to be told that they were the backbone of the nation and the true salvation of France. Ah, monsieur, it is convenient that the French can be ruled through their vanity, but it is exhausting.'

'You have a poor opinion of human nature, sir.'

'I do not despise men, my lord, that is a thing you must never say, and I particularly esteem the French.' He came up very close to George and said quietly, but with great intensity: 'Do you hear that, sir, you must never say that I despise the French.'

'I am very sorry, I did not mean – I fear I have angered you.'

'I was not angry. I am never angry.'

The Citoyenne Bonaparte giggled and said something which George did not quite catch.

'You are pleased to smile, madame.' He went over to her and caught her by the chin and gently moved her face from side to side puckering her little lips so that she looked as if she was sucking a comfit. 'Observe, monsieur, that I am never angry because I have such a good wife, such a faithful wife, a wife who never gives me any cause for jealousy.'

He dropped her chin and turned back to George.

'Anger is a wasteful emotion. I am never angry except when I need to be, then I am angry only up to here.' He drew the palm of his hand across his face, just below the tip of his nose, and indeed the face above that point, the unmarked olive-skinned brow, the fine grey-blue eyes, the pale cheeks – all were as still as marble, while below, the mobile lips continued to talk. What was he talking about now? The possibilities of launching mass invasions by flat-bottomed boats, calculations of winds and tides, how to get the troops ashore, methods of dealing with shore batteries. This was information of the greatest strategic importance, he must relay it instantly to Mr Pitt – or was that exactly what he was intended to do? Did Bonaparte have the slightest intention of crossing the Channel? George was concentrating so hard – his French was little more than adequate – that it was some time before he became conscious of the low noise from the other end of the room, somewhere between a sob and a cough.

'What, are you crying, Josephine?'

'It was only a cough, a tickle in my throat.'

'You are pale this evening, have you forgotten to put on your rouge? Two things are very becoming to women, rouge and tears, don't you think so, milord?'

George bowed in silence, unable to think of a reply.

'You think perhaps that I transgress the *convenances*, monsieur? Well, I must tell you that I do not care for the *convenances*, or for good taste or for any of those social gags that inhibit *l'esprit fort* and play into the hands of the weak. Good taste has been the ruin of France. When I am gone, no doubt the nation will heave a giant sigh of relief and the salons will return to their gossip and their cards and their stupid little affairs. But meanwhile I shall remind them how to live.'

He grinned, a sudden schoolboy conspirator's grin, and George found himself grinning back.

He could not get Bonaparte's grin out of his mind all through the glorious long sun-tanned months that followed. He remembered it as he sat on an Athenian hill looking beyond the long walls and out to sea. His tutor and Cambridge friend, Mr Whittington, had lashed the green umbrella to the stump of the only olive tree in the place, a scrubby thing which afforded no shade. And there they would sit all through the heat of the day, scraping the dirt off the marble tablets which they had found among the stones and thistles of the amphitheatre below. They could see at a glance that these were ex-voto tablets, probably late, Hellenic at best, more likely Roman. They were not as large or as beautiful as the reliefs Lord Elgin had shipped back home the year before, but then Lord Elgin was Ambassador to the Sublime Porte and he George was not yet twenty, but who cared? They were on hallowed ground, the Pnyx, the meeting-place of the Assembly, the Ecclesia – and for them it was as sacred as a church and the birthplace of democracy. And to him had fallen by some mysterious unexpected piece of luck the chance of excavating this holy place. He clambered up and down the steep semi-circular slope, the reddish dust staining his white trousers and sea-blue shirt, with an ecstatic sense of removal from ordinary mortal life. When he cried out to the workmen, a cheerful bunch of Albanian bandits, that they must take care where they dug and sift the spoil with the greatest possible care, he felt he was warning himself against the hubris which came from too much happiness.

He scribbled his notes with the wild rapidity of a man in a laudanum trance. And there was so much to be noted, the condition of the Parthenon, the exact spots where he had found the marble tablets (already packed in straw and waiting for the next Royal Navy frigate to take them back to safekeeping in London), the dimensions of the auditorium and of the huge trapezoidal blocks that made up its colossal retaining wall, and then most sacred of all, just above the rough ground where they had found the tablets, the three-stepped platform, thirty foot wide and twenty foot deep, the Bema, the tribune where Pericles and Demosthenes and Themistocles and Aristides had held their audience. Aristides, the insufferably just, was George's hero, precisely because he was so insufferable, because he pushed on in pursuit of virtue when others were distracted or conceded the odd point to human fallibility. There was something gloriously uncompromising about the idea of Aristides.

Not that George was a prig or a milksop. Sometimes they would walk twenty or thirty miles when the temperature was in the eighties, and in the evening he would leave Whittington to brush up his Menander while he slipped off to the pleasant stucco villa near his lodgings on the outskirts of the city running down to the sea where the harbourmaster and his delightful wife lived with their even more delightful daughter, Catherina, who looked like Josephine must have looked at the age of eighteen and was as free and generous in her affections as Josephine must have been. And she had Josephine's self-mockery too. Down on the beach, she tugged at the buttons of his dusty white trousers with pretend annoyance and combed his curly black hair with her fingers as though he was a tousled dog, and when she told him to stop, somehow the stopping seemed as wonderful as the going on would have been. All the next day, he would still feel the prickling of the shingle on his knees and the palms of his hands and remember the softness of her moans. For the first time in his life, he felt he was fated to be happy. The black dooms that had overtaken his parents would not be inherited.

And that same feeling of invulnerable happiness kept pace with him all year long. It sailed with him up the Sea of Marmara to Constantinople and back again. He felt it shimmering around him as he stared across the Hellespont from Sestos to Abydos and wandered down the long peninsula of Gallipoli, picking his way between the irises and anemones until he was nearly blown off his feet by a boisterous breeze whipping round Cape Helles. And the same breeze followed him all the way home up the coast of Dalmatia and through the canals of Venice and the long poplar avenues of Lombardy and the lavender-scented valleys of Provence, as though all nature was conspiring in his favour from one end of Europe to the other.

Even when, a couple of years later, his envious limping namesake cousin began to make fun of him in verse, he could not help smiling at the recollection of his flawless odyssey.

> First in the oat-fed phalanx shall be seen
> The travelled thane, Athenian Aberdeen . . .

Well, he *had* travelled, and in the realms of gold too, and brought some of the gold back and wasn't ashamed of it either.

Let Aberdeen and Elgin still pursue
The shade of fame through regions of Virtú;
Waste useless thousands on their Phidian freaks,
Misshapen monuments and maimed antiques.

George, you must mind if only a little, his sister said. You need not be ashamed of minding, everyone knows how cruel Lord Byron is. You are in good company to be lampooned by him, I declare I should be ashamed not to be lampooned.

But George genuinely, sincerely did not mind, because by then he had plunged into a torrent of happiness compared with which his Mediterranean odyssey had been a splash in a puddle.

— III —

'Oh you will enjoy Bentley.' Mr Pitt had arranged it and as usual Mr Pitt was right. He had seen with his strange acuteness, which was both cold and somehow feminine, that George needed society. To rub along at Putney with Pitt and his housekeeper-niece was society of a sort. There were some of the opinion that Hester – that queer, tall, shrieking, brilliant macaw of a girl – was company enough on her own with her manic monologues on every subject under the sun. Some dim lordling had timed one of her rants with a fob watch and swore that she had talked uninterrupted for forty-seven minutes at a stretch and he could not for the life of him remember on what, although he knew it was brilliant. But Hester Stanhope was twenty-seven and although Mr Pitt loved her with all his heart, he was well aware how queer she was and how little suited she was for a boy seven years younger who had scarcely known an ordinary home or family.

And so George rode up through the full-leafed woods of Middlesex, past Harrow on its little hill and up the gentle incline of Harrow Weald with its wonderful views of the Thames Valley and the answering Surrey hills beyond. He remembered the rabbits scampering into the brambles at his approach and the deer wheeling away into the thickets of birch and hazel. Looking back through the trees, he could still see the bruised-grey cloud of coalsmoke that laid its dirty coverlet on the city, and yet he was in arcadia. At the gatehouse, to rest his horse, he got off and began to stroll down the winding drive between the low old oak trees.

To his amazement, out from the bushes came a laughing gaggle of persons rigged up in the costume of half a century earlier with powdered wigs and spreading brocade coats such as he had only seen on the stage. The ladies' faces were powdered too and plastered with rouge and beauty spots and they were shrilling and waggling fans and quizzing glasses. And from their midst pranced towards him what he now recognised to be his host, sweating, guffawing, throwing out his lace-cuffed arms in a gesture of almost despairing welcome.

'Oh my dear Lord Aberdeen, how sensible you look. You must change into costume this instant. You are – what is he, Catherine?'

'He is playing Faulkland, papa.'

'The jealous Faulkland. Can you imitate jealousy?'

'I know *The Rivals*, of course, but I have no idea of the lines.'

'Nor have we,' roared Lord Abercorn. 'Costume first, lines later, that is my receipt for theatricals. One only does it for the dressing-up. I feel at home in the fashion of my youth. The modern world is so slow. Come and see my theatre.'

Seizing George's hand and pulling him along as if they were a couple of children, Lord Abercorn shot off through the bushes, knocking away the branches with his free hand as he scampered along on his bandy legs. In a clearing, fifty yards or so from the end of the high classical house stood a little creamy stucco rotunda.

'What do you think, got Wilkins to design it for my capers, quite against the advice of my first two wives, the present Lady Abercorn isn't too enamoured of it either but wives and the theatre never mix, do they, hey?'

'I think it is lovely.'

And it was. It was a light and blithe whirligig of a theatre which seemed to have alighted only for a temporary halt on Stanmore Hill before it would twirl off again across the great valley until it was lost in the pale-blue haze of the downs beyond.

'Now then, get your lines off Mr Scott there, that pink young man looking like a mutton chop, and we shall rehearse after taking a dish of tay, not that I really hold with rehearsals myself, they interfere so with the spontaneity of the true artist. And now adieu.' Lord Abercorn waved an extravagant farewell and galumphed off in the direction of the house.

'Do not believe a word of it,' his daughter said. 'He insists on the highest professional standards.'

George was lost as soon as he saw her, as lost and done for as if the turf had dissolved beneath his feet and his sense of balance had disappeared at the same minute so that he was spinning in a void. She was dark, as dark as the other Catherina and with the same black eyes, but where the other Catherina had been solemn and sensuous together, and curiously distant for all the liberties they had enjoyed lying under the rock, Catherine Hamilton came to him with a brimming, irresistible warmth that left him speechless with happiness after they had exchanged two words.

The words they were exchanging were banal and polite enough. Indeed, they had spoken little except to remark on the beauty of the situation, the afternoon, and how tired Lord Aberdeen must be, having ridden all the way from Putney, and him protesting he was not a bit before his host reappeared from a different gap in the bushes, his sharp blue eyes and sharp long nose twitching with mischief.

'Made friends, have ye? Capital, capital. Mr Pitt speaks very highly of you, very highly indeed. Thinks you may make quite a satisfactory ladies' man. I am an *homme à femmes* myself, always have been, wouldn't you say so, my dear? There is no male company to rival that of the sex.'

'Papa, papa. I have quite abandoned the project of reforming him.'

'She's right, you know. It's a hopeless task. I am incorrigible. But we must not waste precious time, we must prepare. The curtain will rise in two hours' time. Mr Sheridan is expected presently, although he is also expected to be late. There now, there's your copy of the damned text. I can tell you you'll have your work cut out playing with Catherine, finest Lydia Languish since Miss Barsanti according to no less an authority than the playwright himself who was good enough to come and make a nuisance of himself at our re-hearsals.' He chucked George a slim green book and trotted off again into the bushes.

Catherine wiped a delicate sweat-bead from her delicate upper lip – the afternoon was hotter than ever and George felt the sun swatting the back of his neck like the flat of a cricket bat – and she led him round the bushes to a rustic bench where the whole Thames Valley swooned before him in its four o'clock haze.

'Did you ever see such a picturesque spot to learn your lines in?'

'Never,' George said, gulping with panic at the thought of the curtain rising in – it must be only an hour and a half now – and Mr Sheridan spreading his coat-tails as he settled into the front row.

'And now I shall leave you to your task.'

Ah, there was Faulkland's first entrance, much too early for George's liking. The part was full of lines, and not lines that you could easily get a hold on either. 'I had nothing to detain me in Bath, when I had business I went on. Well, what news since I left you? How stand matters between you and Lydia?' Commonplace sentences, they could be stacked in any order, but he had to give the right cue. If he miscued Catherine, she would never forgive him, nor would the besotted old playwright. Come to that, he would never forgive himself. 'When I had finished in Bath, I had no business to detain me.' No, that was wrong. How his head was aching. The cricket bat was tapping on his forehead now. 'My absence may fret her; her anxiety for my return, her fears for me may oppress her gentle temper; and for her health, does not every hour bring me cause to be alarmed?' He would never do it, he would be cast out of this airy arcadia as a stammering idiot.

'Well then, sir, how are you getting on? Perfect are ye?' Lord Abercorn's wheezy bray broke into his frantic rehearsal. Catherine was leaning against her father as though against some rickety tree. She peered at George with almost scientific curiosity.

'I am afraid, sir, that I can't hope to give anything resembling an adequate performance. Is there nobody else here who knows the part at all?'

'Can't Hope To Give An Adequate Performance. I never heard of such a thing. Catherine, did you ever hear of such a thing?'

'Certainly not, papa, never.'

'Two whole days to rehearse in, and the fellow can't promise to be adequate.'

'Days, did you say, sir, days?'

'Of course I said days.'

'But the first time you said hours, I'm sure of it, you said hours.'

'Did I really? Did I now? I forget.' Lord Abercorn stared vaguely at the view — and then collapsed into unfeeling laughter, joined by his daughter, so that between the two of them they convulsed like a concertina.

George at first was nettled by the trick — he was easily nettled, always had been since he was a proud little child — then the relief overcame him and he joined in the laughter, uneasily at first, but soon he was swept away by the delight of father and daughter. Catherine was laughing so much that the corners of her bright eyes were wet with tears.

'Oh you looked so anxious . . . .'

'. . . and he was muttering so hard, muttering like a mussulman.'

'We were watching from the bushes. It was agony, perfect agony.'

George began to be nettled again by the thought of being spied on, then was swept away once more as they put him between them, linked arms and took him off for a dish of tay as Lord Abercorn kept on calling it in his somewhat suspect imitation of the accents of the age of Queen Anne. In all his life, George reflected, nobody had ever linked arms with him, and the self-pity at the thought of his loneliness only gilded his happiness.

To everybody's surprise – for he was well aware how stiff a figure he cut in company – George turned out to be a creditable Faulkland full of jealous fire.

Lord Abercorn, in his fantastic-generous style, was quick to pay tribute. 'You expostulate handsomely, sir, you are a grand expostulator.' And Catherine threw him admiring smiles as she danced her way through the part of Lydia Languish with a negligent charm that suggested she had improvised the lines herself.

The weather had broken by the evening of the performance, and George was glad of his green umbrella as they tiptoed through the drizzle along the gravel walk to the rotunda. Catherine sheltered under his umbrella arm. He could hardly speak for nerves. The fragrance of her scent, delicate though it was, seemed suffocating in the heavy air. He had a certainty – sudden and overwhelming – that they would never be parted till death. He was overjoyed and terrified.

The little pink and gold auditorium with its steeply raked red velvet seats was nearly full: neighbouring gentry and the non-acting guests at the Priory in the front, servants and tenantry in the upper rows. In the front row, there was an empty space. Mr Sheridan had not come.

'He'll have mistaken the day.'

'Or the place. At this very minute he'll be breaking the door down at Stanmore Rectory.'

'Well, we won't wait for Sheridan. We'd be here until September.'

In fact, the play had been under way for no more than half an hour when a rheumy elderly gentleman stumbled across the feet of the guests in the front row. He staggered and seemed certain to fall into the flares lining the front of the stage, then with an extravagant gesture of terror probably unequalled since Garrick's Macbeth he regained his balance and pitched into his seat like an old man falling into bed. For some minutes he lay askew as he had fallen, then sat himself upright with a violent shake of his shoulders. From the stage, George felt a pair of bloodshot but penetrating blue eyes fixed on him and began with alarm to notice that the purple lips were beginning to move in time with the lines. Then all was well again. Mrs Malaprop, played by a jovial dowager whose name George was still not quite sure of, was getting into her stride. And every time she uttered a mangled word or phrase, their author gave a manic clucking chuckle, not unlike a bird disturbed from its nest. By the end of the scene, he was rolling around in his seat clutching his neighbour's arm, slapping his thigh again and again, then slapping *her* thigh, and then as the actors retired, rising in his seat and bellowing, Bravo, bravo. At the end of the play, he rushed forward as though intending to throw himself upon the flares and raised his hands high and wide to the actors in a gesture of admiration and triumph, gathering the panting, exhausted cast to him, then turned to the audience, repeating the gesture, gathering *them* to him, so that the whole of the little rotunda was enfolded in the enthusiastic embrace of Richard Brinsley Sheridan. It was a moment that George was never to forget.

'Was not that marvellous,' Catherine whispered to him, as they were about to separate to change out of their costumes. 'Papa swore that if Mr Sheridan were to make an appearance at all he would fall fast asleep the moment he sat down and we should count ourselves lucky if he did not snore and drown the actors.'

'You were wonderful, Lady Catherine.'

'Oh Catherine, you must call me Catherine, and you were not entirely disgraceful yourself, my lord.'

She gave him a light kiss, as light as the brushing of a blade of grass, and skipped off to the house where the ladies had their greenroom. George strolled in a daze towards the gentlemen's changing tent. The rain had stopped now, the moon had come out, cold and clear in the misty sky. He could see the lights of London over the edge of the hill.

He became aware of a man standing with his back to him in front of the bushes behind the tent. The man was relieving himself. The moonlight caught the droopy arc of his piss and the silver brocade of his lapels.

Without any warning, the man uttered a long sigh. It was an appealing sound, sodden with fatigue and despair, it seemed to go on for an eternity. Then he was silent, and George could just hear the faint whistle of his piss again. Then the man spoke, in a high hollow voice, a stagey sort of voice.

'Amateurs!' he said.

The sound of the pissing died away, and Mr Sheridan began to button himself up with a good deal of tugging and wrenching and swearing.

In the great hall of the Priory Lord Abercorn, still in costume as Sir Anthony Absolute, was dispensing punch, splashing his cuffs with impatient scoops of the silver ladle.

'Well, my lord, ye can tell your grandchildren that ye acted before Mr Sheridan.'

'I rather think, my lord, that Mr Sheridan acted before us.'

Lord Abercorn paused in mid-scoop, his sharp nose twitching like a fox's snout. He was instantly beguiled by the thought.

'Oh, ye think he hated it, do ye? All that bravoing just for show? I'm sure you're right. Sherry!'

And to George's horror, the decayed, distracted but not inelegant figure of Mr Sheridan shambled over towards them. In the full light of the hall, the watery twinkle in his eye and the laughing twist of his mouth utterly made light of all his misfortunes.

'Never, my Lord Abercorn, in the history of the

British drama has such grace, such wit, such professional dexterity adorned so poor a play. If I die tonight, I shall die a fulfilled and happy creature to have seen my feeble words so bravely articulated by such a noble and talented cast.'

'You didn't think much of the performance then?'

'My dear sir, I am giddy with delight, I am utterly, hopelessly intoxicated. If you give me so much as a drop of that no doubt unparalleled punch, I shall collapse in a stupor.'

'In that case, perhaps it would be wiser if I stayed my hand.'

'Wiser, my lord, but not kinder. On second thoughts, I rather fancy that a bumper or two might act in the nature of a restorative. I am played out, sir, quite played out. My word, this punch is ambrosial, and not a clove in it. I can't abide that rectory punch, you go to bed cold sober and have to spend half the night spitting cloves out of your teeth. Been to France, I hear, saw Boney too, they tell me."

'Yes sir,' George stammered, taken aback by this attention.

'Charmed you, I expect. He charms everybody when he wants to, charmed poor old Fox, you know. They're all charmers, these tyrants, precisely because nobody's expecting it. We come in with our knees knocking, there he sits on his throne looking like the wrath of God, knees knock twice as hard, then what does he do, he *smiles*, doesn't matter if he hasn't a tooth in his head or his breath smells like a barrel of rotten fish, he smiles and we are lost.'

'He does have a most beguiling smile.'

'There you are, you see. Lost. I tell you what, sir, we won't be quiet until we're rid of him. I'm drilling the volunteers every morning in St. James's Park, eight o'clock sharp.'

'Drilling . . .'

'Yes, sir, drilling' – and then Mr Sheridan broke out into the most entrancing, theatrical laugh like a whole herd of horses whinnying and began to describe how he put the St. James's volunteers through their paces, a process which seemed to require as props an ingenious collapsible canvas stool and a brandy flask disguised as a telescope.

'Like Lydia hiding *The Innocent Adultery* in *The Whole Duty of Man*.'

'Quite, quite, oh I did enjoy the play, sir. Such talent, such fizz, what an author. I wish I could write like that.'

'I trust that we may soon see another –'

'Oh tush, comedy's a young man's game, and there's enough tragedies in the world without adding to them.' A cloud of melancholy invaded Mr Sheridan's features and veiled that sharp pointed aspect George had observed when he was talking of Bonaparte.

That was not the only play George acted in, that unforgettable summer. Three or four times he rode up through the thickets of oak and hazel, pausing for a mug of cider at the crooked little inn in the woods, before geeing his horse up the last steep incline to Bentley where Lord Abercorn would be waiting on the steps tossing him his script as he was dismounting.

'*Oroonoko*? What's that?' George said bending to pick the flimsy volume up off the gravel.

'What, don't ye know Mrs Behn's improving tale? Southerne adapted it for Drury Lane and playgoers have wept tears enough at it to launch a man o' war. And you, my dear Lord Aberdeen, are to have the plum, Oroonoko, the slave Prince of Angola. You enter in chains, you die in chains, you have the most fetching costume – black silk arms and leggings, red sandals, golden belt and bracelets and coronet. There was never a part like it. And you have my daughter Catherine as your princess. She's white, you're black, of course, we have the burnt cork ready. It is a most edifying play, full of fine sentiments, and you have the pick of the speeches, my lord.'

He did, and he made the most of them. On stage, he found a reckless confidence such as only the shy have access to. He rolled his dark eyes and adopted a limber African gait and a hoarse passionate way with the pentameters. But then he had no need to simulate passion with his white-skinned Princess Imelda clanking her chains as she threw herself into his arms.

Let the fools who follow fortune live upon her
  smiles.
All our prosperity is placed in love.
We have enough of that to make us happy.
This little spot of earth you stand upon
Is more to me than the extended plains
Of my great father's kingdom.

That was no less than the truth. He loved not only her
whiteness and her flashing eye. Her proud temper
answered his own. They had been reared in the same
hard school. Her mother had died when she was
twelve, Lord Abercorn's second marriage had turned
out a conspicuous disaster and had been dissolved by
Act of Parliament, and Catherine's second stepmother
was no less difficult. He loved her particularly as she
stood with her head turned away in scorn and loathing
when the Prince of Wales, out of breath and more than
a little squiffy, insisted on fastening an armlet above
her white elbow.

'You did not care for that much.'

'I had rather die in chains with you, my lord.'

'That would be a concatenation devoutly to be
wished.'

'Was that a pun, my lord? If so, I advise against it. I
hate puns.'

'In that case, I shall deluge you with them until you
surrender.'

'I never surrender, my lord, I merely elude capture.'

And so it went on, as natural as the little stream

which tripped down through the woods and ran into the Silk Stream and then tipped into the Brent and then into the Thames at Brentford and so on down to the sea. They were married the following July in the Jacobean church at the bottom of the hill with its rose red tower and crumbling mullions. It was not all romance, of course. Lord Abercorn suddenly displayed a decidedly earthy streak and insisted that his daughter be 'maintained in the style of splendour she had always been us'd to, which was proper for her rank in life'. George's own brothers and sisters panicked and insisted that their own portions be safeguarded and he also had a debt of honour to his old curator Melville, now disgraced and bust. But somehow he wriggled through these financial entanglements, and through August and September they embraced all night and much of the day too. They played spillikins with their arms about each other's necks, and when they were walking in the thickest parts of the hazel woods their hands sought and found each other's bodies like squirrels frolicking up a tree trunk.

She would stroke the back of his neck while he sat composing his learned articles on classical antiquity, with a little smile twitching the corner of his monkey mouth. The article pouring scalding scorn on poor Gell's *Topography of Troy*, for example. Who in his right mind could confuse the miserable village of Bournabaski with the site of Troy or identify the source of the mighty Scamander with the miserable local ditch? He had seen the true source himself: 'The water rises in a vast cavern of white marble and gushes out by two apertures in the rock forming in its fall a magnificent cascade; and the surrounding precipices being covered with pine, oak and plane trees, render the whole scene eminently beautiful and imposing.' And as for Monsieur Dutens's absurd contention that the arch had been in use among both the Greeks and the Egyptians from the second millennium BC, he minced Monsieur Dutens to nothingness: everywhere the traveller sees a true arch – Ephesus, Miletus, Magnesia, Troas, Alexandria – he will find that it is Hellenistic or Roman work.

'Everywhere, my lord?' Catherine kissed his ear.

'Everywhere. Apsis, tholos – none of these terms implies a true arch. Barrel vaults, yes, or even the sort of thing children make with overlapping stones, but never a true arch, not before the time of Alexander the Great.'

'Poor Monsieur Dutens.'

'I shall incorporate an outline of the argument in my Inquiry into the Principles of Beauty in Grecian Architecture. I am carrying forward the speculations of Mr Burke on the subject.'

'And do I conform to your principles?'

'The essay is confined to architecture. I may find room for you in a footnote.'

'Only a footnote, my lord?'

'You will look very pretty in a footnote.'

'I should prefer to be remembered on an arch – in bas relief, I think. Or perhaps on an urn. Yes, I should like an urn.'

'Let me show you what I mean.' He led her out to the stable yard and the little lean-to shed in the corner where the estate mason kept his stones, bricks and tiles. He dragged a supply of flat and wedge-shaped stones out into the uneven cobbles and began to build.

'There, this is how it is at Mycenae.' The long overlapping stones wobbled as they met and then dipped in a dismal shallow v. As he stood back from them, they slowly collapsed on the cobbles.

'But not in Middlesex, it seems.'

'Whereas', he continued unmoved, 'a true arch grips itself securely.' He knelt down on the grass-grown cobbles and began to construct a true arch, but could not find a decent keystone.

'Oh my darling lord, I do know what an arch is. I am, after all, the daughter of a fanatical amateur architect.'

'Catherine, you must always tell when I become preachy. It is a congenital fault, I am aware of it, but it takes hold of me.'

'But I married you for your preachiness. I declare I should be at my wits' end if you lost it.'

She even liked Scotland, thought of it as a northern arcadia and wrote from Haddo to her difficult, anxious father (who was almost in love with George himself but was still capable of making trouble):

Dear Papa,
You need not believe one word of what Lord Aberdeen says about this place, for I assure you that there is nothing to complain of. I never was so surprised in my life as when I first saw it, for I had been told so much about it by everybody, that I expected a thing not fit for a human being to live in, placed in the middle of a barren, bleak moor without a tree or anything near it but a bog. Instead of that I saw a great many very good trees about the house, which is not regularly beautiful on the outside but very comfortable on the inside, from the windows you see nothing but trees, with a good chair and sopha or two and new curtains to the drawing-room. I do not wish for anything better – and what do you think, I have got two little tame fawns.

They only went north in the summer, but the summer afternoons and evenings seemed endless. She sat under the green umbrella in the new plantations while he helped the men clear the ground and dig the holes for the saplings which they were planting by the thousand, fir and oak and ash and hazel and larch, and nearer the house a few exotics for the delectation of the dendrophile. He kept a tally of his planting and sent it to his father-in-law who would reply in kind: Larch 195,000, Scotch Fir 444,000, Oak 10,200. The young trees stretched away to the horizon, muzzy swathes of pale green and unripe lemon which turned greeny-blue as the sun, with some reluctance, lowered itself over Formartine. When they had planted enough for the day, George and Catherine would swing up on to the horses which had been cropping the grass on the side of the rabbit fence and amble down the rides that had been made through the plantations down to the lake. They rode side by side, stirrup brushing stirrup, hands now and then interlaced, until George, seeing a crooked young sapling, would hop off and attend to it. He was burnt as black as he had been when excavating the Pnyx, and even Catherine's white skin had a rosy-brown flush. Like a branch of blackberries we are, she said to one of the parlour maids, who had the same black eyes as she had. And soon the house was fuller still – the coy allusion must be excused, the spectacle of their happiness unmans the sternest narrator. Jane was born the following year, Caroline a year later, and Alice the year after that – tumbling black-eyed monkeys who were soon chasing one another down the long soft-grassed rides between the saplings that were scarcely taller than they were. George watched it all with disbelief. That the dry and stony wastes of his youth could have blossomed so abundantly – not merely did he not believe it, but there was a melancholy, sceptical part of him which never ceased to mutter that he would have to pay for it all. Meanwhile, he watched: Catherine's long white body moving beneath him with its strange rhythm, so far and yet so near, and then moving differently, contorted with pain and effort and then flooded with exhaustion and delight – he was very near her at the moment of birth, perhaps even present, he did not want to miss anything. And then the smells – in retrospect it was the smells of the first years of marriage that stayed longest in his odd sensual yet abstracted mind: the milky smell of the babies, the delicate sourness of their napkins, the light flowery smell of Catherine's cologne, the coconut smell of the gorse, the sweet resin of the pine forest where the capercailzie still roosted like aerial turkeys.

That winter he took his seat in the House of Lords. Not a painless process. To start with, he had to get elected as a representative Scottish peer, for he had no English peerage, and the Scotch peers wangled and havered and haggled like Arab merchants. They switched votes with bewildering rapidity, slid out of unbreakable commitments, ratted at the whiff of a better offer. As soon as you had Glasgow, Napier and Reay in the bag, Cathcart and Dundonald would defect, Mair was dubious, Belhaven was unobtainable, Torphichen was mad. At the end of the queerest proceedings known to man, he barely scraped in and plumped down on the Tory benches with a sigh of relief. But the next hurdle was higher still. He was averse to spouting in public, and unpractised in the black art, that much he knew about himself, but quite how averse and how unpractised he had not fully realised until he began rehearsing his maiden speech. It was to be in favour of the abolition of the Slave Trade, a measure which the Ministry of All the Talents had prepared in the pleasant anticipation of demonstrating their own unity in the face of a divided opposition. The words were fine and judicious, the tone measured, the arguments deliciously balanced. He went over them again and again. 'My lords, this abominable trade has for too long desecrated . . .' but even with no larger audience than the pier-glass in his bedroom, he could not spit them out with any semblance of conviction. He sounded mumbling and furtive, more like a burglar up before the beak than an embryo statesman. And the more he rehearsed, the more the words failed him: 'This amominable trade has desiccated . . .'

On the day of the debate, with a megrim banging at his skull, he trudged across the floor of the House like a man going to his execution. As he passed in front of the steps of the throne, he found a couple of sturdy legs in white stockings barring his way.

'How d'ye do, Haddock, going to amaze us this afternoon, are ye?'

'Cupid.'

'Lord Palmerston, if you please. We poor Irish peers may only be permitted to sit at your feet, but we do like to be properly addressed.'

'You were elected to the other place, were you not, last month?'

'In a manner of speaking. The petition is not decided yet. I've paid fifteen hundred pounds at least for the privilege of a fortnight in the House. Meanwhile, I am improving the shining hour by taking a lesson in rhetoric from my betters.'

There was a grin on his pink face, a silly, oafish young-blood's grin, a grin which betrayed utter indifference to the fate of toiling slaves in the sugar plantations, or indeed to any cause except the cause of amusing and advancing Harry Temple.

George chose a seat at the back. He began to feel queasy as soon as the debate began. Every time his eyes wandered beyond the speakers, he saw young Lord Palmerston's white legs sprawling over the steps and young Lord Palmerston's insolent face under its mop of tousled hair. Another young lout in full fig came and sat down on the red carpet beside Cupid. They began whispering and laughing and nodding in George's direction, he was sure of it. A queer rippling sort of pain ran right across George's stomach, from his lower ribs right down to his groin.

'Are you all right, my lord?' The sandy-faced peer sitting next to him had a faintly Scottish voice. George could not remember which of them it was – Napier was it, or Belhaven? – and whether they had voted for one another. The chamber was so vilely hot. The tapers seemed to flicker in unison.

'I feel a little . . . Is there a . . .?' The sandy-faced Scot gestured to a little door in the wall behind them.

George got up and scuttled out. It was four months before he spoke for the first time in that place, and twenty years before he made a decent speech there.

They travelled too, paid visits to relations, took lodgings at Brighton for the sea air and watched the babies crawl over the shingle and flop down on the sand like tired jellyfish. Catherine was pregnant again and this time she seemed peaky and even a little feverish. Her brother too had not been well and was also staying in Brighton with *his* pregnant wife who was due to be confined a month later. All should have been rosy, but Catherine's brother remained poorly and George did not care for Harriet. 'She is rather well looking, as you know,' he wrote to his brother Alec (serving with Wellington out in Spain), 'but certainly one of the most stupid persons I ever met with.'

Then for no apparent reason, without warning, Catherine had a miscarriage and lost the child, a son (and heir, but he put that out of his mind), half an hour after his birth. Catherine was weak and stayed weak. Her tubercular tendency, identified years earlier and fretted over by her devoted distracted father ever since, seemed to take hold of her. She was not in pain, even her cough was only a slight, almost apologetic thing, but her pulse fluttered like the wings of a butterfly and she had no strength at all. By the end of December, they had four doctors including Knighton the royal physician attending on her, none of them able to tell George anything but the obvious, which was that she was suffering from an inflammation of the lungs. Sometimes she was gay and lively in company, and the flush on her cheeks was like the flush she could not prevent when teasing him at the Priory on their first meeting. But at other times, when she was tired and the company had gone but the flush still lingered, her face had an almost crazed aspect. Her arm stretching up from under the bedclothes for the glass of water on her bedside table seemed so white and skeletal. He could not help thinking of those terrible matchstick figures painted on the walls of the cloister at Pisa, the *danse macabre*, and he desperately tried to chase the thought out of his mind. His brother wrote again from Spain complaining that George never wrote to him and George replied with some irritation: 'The fact is, I seldom write to anyone, except frequent accounts of Lady Aberdeen to her parents. Her health is in such a state that I am obliged to attend to her nearly all day, and when not actually occupied with her, it is not easy for me to think of anything else. She is much the same as she has been for some time past, but frequent bleedings have made her very weak.' Distracted, and edging closer and closer to despair, he sent for a doctor from Scotland who was said to have worked wonders. But the wonder-worker, a short, gingery man with huge tufts of hair in his ears, had nothing fresh to say and said it in a grating Aberdonian voice that George found intolerable. He sent all the doctors away except one and settled down to face what he now knew he had to face and cursed himself for not facing earlier, and for not having been more patient with her complaints the autumn before.

She died on Leap Year's Day. For several days she had been so weak that her dying seemed only the slightest of transitions, but for him the distance was huge. His own physical strength – his muscles hardened by tree-planting eight hours a day, by walking twenty miles or riding thirty at a stretch – all that seemed like a reproach. The next day, when he was making funeral arrangements with Mr Crombie, he heard that Napoleon might be planning to march on Russia, and his rage mixed with his grief was so intense that he had to shoo Mr Crombie out of the morning-room to be able to groan and curse and weep on his own. His tears salted his snuff-brown sleeve and he realised with a kind of sacred horror that he had no black clothes with him in London, and he rushed out into the pouring rain and ran with frantic strides to his tailor in the little street behind Burlington House.

'You're wet, soaking through, my lord,' the tailor said, after promising that his cutters would work through the night and call in the morning for a fitting (meanwhile, there was a mourning suit which had been returned under circumstances best forgotten which would fit him tolerably and which he could borrow). 'You're wet through,' he repeated, mesmerised by the dark young man whose eyes were red with weeping. 'You must take my umbrella after you've changed.'

And so having put on his borrowed weeds which smelled unpleasantly of coal-tar and nipped him round the armpits, George took the discreet black umbrella, scarcely able to form words to thank the tailor, and walked off into the rain. Although he was a great walker in London, he had never walked like this before with the rain and the tears in his eyes, driving his legs along through the mud of the building work that stretched halfway to the Prince Regent's new park, and then on beyond past Tom Lord's cricket ground and up along the side of Hampstead Heath, past the Spaniards Inn, and the gloomy house where the elder Pitt had gone mad in old age and on up the long straight road to Edgware and then through the bare branches and rivulets of mud and dead leaves up the hill to Bentley. On his little finger he wore the ring he had taken from her finger on her deathbed, and he felt it tight on the joint as he stared at the shuttered windows. He did not know why he had come. His father-in-law and the rest of the family were down in town. What was he there for? To catch the first glimpse of her ghost?

That glimpse came soon enough without his having to go looking for it. It was a blustery spring night at Haddo, he had come up to settle some minor estate matters, and the wind was keeping him awake. Without any warning, he saw her come in through the door, dressed to go out riding (or tree-planting or mushroom-picking) with an impatient look on her face, as though to say, 'Come on, the horses are saddled in the yard,' but she said nothing, just walked on through the bedroom and then was no longer there.

'*Vidi,*' he wrote in his journal, in the safe obscurity of Latin.

A month later he saw her for a second time in his study in London, again dressed for riding, but the vision was briefer and fainter.

'*Vidi sed obscuriorem,*' he wrote.

The next vision was more substantial, much more. He was in his study again, reading a letter which had been sent to him in his new capacity as a trustee of the British Museum, and there she was sitting opposite him in her rose-madder summer dress with her dark hair escaping down her neck and smiling that smile she smiled after they had been happy together.

'*Verissima, dulcissima imago,*' he wrote.

And then finally at Haddo that summer, one evening after he had thrown himself down on his bed – he had driven his body to the limit, he had been planting trees since first light – she came to him and stayed.

'*Tota nocti vidi, ut in vita.*'

This was the last vision, but never a day, probably never an hour passed without his thinking of her, and he wore black for the rest of his life (a habit of grief which made him look like a Scotch minister and was somewhat resented in society). Naturally the umbrella he carried from then on was also black.

He woke from these visions exhausted and wretched, his nightshirt wet with sweat. But his body was not quite consumed by grief. When he had bathed and shaved, he would feel a sharp reminder of the flesh, a stab of unextinguished desire. He could not keep his eyes off the little black-eyed girl he had brought down from Haddo, as she served the devilled kidneys. On his way through Soho, he would see the gay women with their baskets under their arms off to the German grocer in Brewer Street, chatting away like respectable matrons, and he would dawdle, letting his eye linger on the sway of their hips. Perhaps, his sober self would murmur to him, Argyll House was not a suitable address for a man of his character, perhaps he should move to St. James's. But he did not move. He liked the smell of the coffee and the Indian spices and the Italian violinist with the monkey and the one-legged veteran of Quebec who drew portraits in chalk in Golden Square. What he needed was – well, he knew what he needed, but he did not care to define it. He had, as he put it to his sister-in-law Maria, known the most perfect creature ever formed by the power and wisdom of God. He could not, would not pollute that memory by a quick coupling in a squalid lodging two streets away. But he must start afresh.

There was, for a start, his sister-in-law. Maria had the same bright dark eyes as Catherine, the same flash and wit and exuberance, the same rush of affection too. She was a consolation, a confidante, a temporary mother to his children. Their friends were convinced that she was more to him than that, but she was also his deceased wife's sister, and under the law then as forbidden to him as if she were his own sister. And George – how can one say this without exposing him to your ridicule? – had a law-abiding imagination.

So he wrote to Maria as if she were an old schoolfriend and there was not an ounce of desire in their relationship. He described how he had been to supper at Devonshire House after the opera – the ices melting under the candelabra, the wine not chilled – and sat down next to Anne Cavendish under the frosty eyes of Lady Holland and Lady Harrowby, who disapproved of Whigs and Tories mixing. 'Anne continued to talk with great empressement on very interesting subjects, charming and catching me in an unusual manner. This was the more difficult as from the small size of the table it was necessary to do it almost in a whisper, and she seemed to wish not to be heard -- you may believe that I did my best; and I am quite certain with effect, her look and manner incontestably evinced it. I do not recollect that I ever made a greater exertion. Now is not all this most extraordinary? I never can believe that she is playing the heartless game of a regular coquette. It is impossible – what am I to think? Lady H. talks a great deal to my brother about my marrying, and blames my notions of a *mariage de convenance*. Of course, I have no such motives, but if Anne understands my views in this way, I do not wonder at her reluctance or that of her family. This should be cleared up. I feel capable of entertaining sentiment for her more ardent and pure than I believe she is likely to meet with. Most undoubtedly, as long as I live, I shall believe that I have seen human nature under a form in which it never before existed. My heart must be more than meta-phorically cold before this feeling can be changed or forgotten. Yet if I am not wholly mistaken in the character of Anne, she will not have to complain of any want of enthusiasm and devotion. Tell, my dear Lady Maria, what am I to do?'

We do not know what Lady Maria told him to do, still less what she thought of her brother-in-law and how garrulous and effusive she had become since he had been a widower. Even less can we guess at what she thought of his passionate, almost religious devotion to her dead sister. After all, if you had grown up with Catherine, you could not help remembering her scorching temper and her delight in taking the wings off a daddy-long-legs, in twisting her younger sisters' plump little arms, and in making fun of stiff young men. Perhaps Maria did not dwell much on what was past; she had enough to do looking after George's three little girls, Jane, Caro and Alice, administering calomel, James's powder and salts for their weak chests, and pasting down the rackety windows of Argyll House with strong brown paper to keep out the draughts. We don't know how Maria felt about having to do all this or what she wanted or hoped for out of her life for, despite her high spirits, she was too well-bred to say at the time and there was no time after for recollection, because she died two years later, without being married and without reaching thirty.

In any case, Anne Cavendish, choosy, tricky Anne, would not have George. Naturally, he blamed the two Lady H.s for poisoning her mind against him, but then he could not see himself as others saw him at that time. He had a wild look which estranged his monkey face and took away its endearing quality. And he talked so much. Old gentlemen in Brooks's were unnerved by this strange, fierce-looking young man who button-holed and deluged them with conversation on topics that frightened them – had the Greeks discovered the arch? the proper nature of democracy, how to control the lava flow from a volcano. When he talked about trees they began to relax, but even then he went on too long and into too much detail – the germination period of the poplar in north-east Scotland, for example. Loneliness began to hang about him like fog, and when he strode home with that tireless yet lumbering gait, even the gay women coming out for the evening would hesitate before going up to him. There was a strength about him, but there was a load of sorrow too, and the combination made him odd. No, he was more alarming than that, he was weighed down by a tragic sense which was never to leave him, and sensible people can detect a tragic sense from a hundred yards away and will cross the street to avoid brushing against it and catching something.

— IV —

He had refused enough.
They had wanted him to go as British Minister in
Sicily and he would not. He had turned down the
Embassy in Moscow. And then when she was dying,
he had refused to go to Washington. Even now, when
they were pressing him to go to Vienna – or wherever
the Emperor was – and make peace in Europe, he did
not want to leave his three little motherless girls. But
he was twenty-nine and proud and eager. Action
could only help break up the louring cloud of grief.
And his sister-in-law Maria, the nearest thing left on
earth to the most perfect creature ever formed by the
power and wisdom of God, she would look after Jane
and Caro and Alice, but she must be told not 'to spoil
them, not to let them be stuffed with eatables of any
sort or admired to their faces'. He laid down stiff terms

for his mission, and his father-in-law egged him on: 'You are perfectly right stipulating to be Nulli Secundus in any scene or transaction of your Embassy. An undisguised personal and national haughtiness (with a sweet sauce of studied, unremitting, ceremonious, condescending politeness and attention) is much more advantageous than is guessed.' He could manage the haughtiness well enough, Catherine had teased him about his Scotch pride. About the unremitting politeness he was less confident.

But he was tough and he needed to be. He had searing headaches and recurring rampant diarrhoea amounting to *cholera morbus*. One night on the road to Prague – or rather the muddy filthy track to Prague: the passage of the Russian troops and artillery had destroyed any claims to call it a road – the carriage overturned and they stood in the rain for four hours with only a few stumps of fir trees for shelter and two crusts of dry bread between them. The next morning, the rain had cleared and they heard a clatter of horses coming up behind them. George peered out of the coach and saw the most astonishing sight: several hundred Asiatical Tartars, armed with bows and arrows, and carrying light spears. 'They have the Chinese face and are exactly like the fellows one sees painted on tea-boxes,' he wrote to Maria (who else was he to write to now?). They passed him in silence, sitting on their short-legged horses, little more than ponies, only the clacking of the arrows in their boxy wooden quivers, and the slush and slap of the hooves in the mud disturbing the damp Silesian dawn.

'Our gallant Russian allies,' he remarked to the dozy curly head of his secretary Fred Lamb, which had poked out of the carriage window alongside him.

'They frighten the life out of me, at any rate,' Fred said in that drawly Lamb voice and then flopped back inside the carriage.

Even when they reached Prague, they discovered that they had not come to the end of their long circuitous odyssey (by boat to Gothenburg, then across Sweden by land and over the Baltic to Stralsund and down through Pomerania to Berlin). For the Emperor and Metternich had gone on north to join the army, and they must follow. At first, they jogged along through rolling countryside which put him in mind of the prosperous tracts of the Highlands with its little woods of oak and birch and self-sown fir trees dotted about the easy slopes. Then, not long after they had passed through Theresienstadt, where the road bent round the smart new red-brick fortress with its bulgy towers like a child's toy fortress, not long after that, they began to see. Fred was wide awake now.

The first wagon was lying half on, half off the grassy bank to the left of the road. It was an old farm cart, once painted red, now covered with mud. They heard the groans first, long muttering wails breaking out into coughs and then into low sobbing groans again. One or two of the corpses were neatly piled in a corner of the cart, but the rest were tumbled in with the wounded and dying. There must have been twenty or thirty men on the cart. The driver was vomiting in the ditch. The horses were cropping the grass. As they came closer, the smell overwhelmed them; it was the foulest smell he had ever known, sourer and more poisonous and sweeter than any dung or privy. George retched up the dry bread and water which was all they had had to eat for twenty-four hours. Half a mile down the road, Fred did the same. He sat pale green in the face and refused to look out of the window until he had recovered his calm.

The whole of that day, they passed the wounded, the dead and dying, some of them not yet gathered up into the wagons and crying out for help from the roadside, crawling into the path of their carriage through the puddles of mud and excrement. As the carriage rounded the bend, their cries could still be heard for several miles. 'The shock, and disgust, and pity produced by such scenes are beyond what I could have supposed possible at a distance,' he wrote to Maria from Teplitz. 'There are near two hundred thousand men round this town. There is much splendour and much animation in the sight, yet the scenes of distress and misery have sunk deeper in my mind. I have been quite haunted by them.

'I have seen the Emperor, and have been received as Ambassador. In an audience of considerable length I have had every reason to be satisfied with him.

'God bless you, dearest Lady Maria. Take care of the dear children.'

How many other diplomats before or after him had had such an initiation, such a blooding? He arrived at the pretty little spa town of Teplitz on its tump of a hill with his credentials smeared in the foulest secretions of war. He bowed his frigid Athenian best, dined at the Emperor's table night after night, made friends with Metternich, sly foxy silky Metternich whom perversely George liked and trusted from the first because Metternich never let him down, unlike the scheming bad-tempered British ambassadors to Prussia and Russia, who resented an untried whippersnapper taking precedence over them. Cathcart was lazy and secretive. Stewart was deaf, short-sighted and impetuous. Both mistrusted Austria and hated to see the Emperor flatter the unlicked cub and stroke its fur. Aberdeen would let Metternich make a soft peace and leave Europe still at Napoleon's mercy. Aberdeen kept on talking about moderation, a word which should not have sullied the lips of a British ambassador after such splendid Allied victories. And besides, Aberdeen could not really speak French at all.

The dreadful duo hated to let him out of their sight for fear he should snatch a few minutes of private conversation with 'their' sovereigns. He caught sight of their crapulous English faces – all pop eyes and whiskers – down the table at the banquets in the Spa assembly room, while he, George, was seated next to the Emperor Francis, often with the Russian Emperor Alexander on his other side; their medals gently clanked as they swapped politesses, and the fragrance of their cologne protested against the bad-eggs smell of the waters which made the low-ceilinged room seem even more oppressive.

The hall was not big enough to entertain three sovereigns and their entourages, and the knives and plates had to be heaped together as though in a saleroom, and when George leant forward to catch the imperial quips his forehead brushed the branches of the great silver epergnes which had been lugged all the way from Vienna. And the sweet Rhenish wine sent the megrims thudding up and down his right temple. Metternich too suffered from the most *affreuse migraine*, and they relaxed in the little pink-and-yellow card room by discussing their health.

The thudding was worse in the morning. He needed to clear his head with a stroll, and went down the dusty circular staircase in his mean lodgings and along the dark narrow lane to the square with its high Plague Column, all swirling clouds and angels, not at all in good taste by George's lights, he was not one for this facile Bohemian prettiness. Just beyond the square, he caught sight of some feathery green trees above a crumbling ochre wall. Following the lane down, he found a doorway with faded cherubs sculpted above it, and an old green door half open. He went in to find a decayed formal garden with ragged box hedges in a knot pattern and unweeded gravel paths dotted with little white daisies. In the September morning – the air was heavy in Teplitz, thick and damp with a horrible insinuating smell – the garden had a still and desolate charm. He wandered down the main alley, little more than an overgrown path, under the sticky lime trees which, towards the end of the garden, were overgrown with brambles and wild hazel bushes. At the far wall, he could see a tumbledown summerhouse with a pointed roof and peeling green wooden latticework between the pillars. Below these lattice arches, there were untidy piles of logs. The logs were strange looking, some almost white like stripped birch, others a reddish purple which he could not identify. As he came closer, he saw that they were not logs at all but arms and legs which had been thrown out of the summerhouse. He peered in for a moment before he had to turn away to vomit. The summerhouse seemed to have been used as an operating theatre, with the low green bench used as the surgeon's table and black with blood.

He described the summerhouse in a letter to his friend Harrowby, ending bitterly: 'This is a pleasant incident, of a more interesting nature than you are likely to meet with in your walks at Sandon. The wonder is how we exist at all in this vile hole, with scarcely anything to eat, and that of the worst kind. Surrounded by such multitudes of the living and the dead, human and brute, the air is pestilential. Novice as I am in the scenes of destruction, the continual sight of the poor wounded wretches of all nations is quite horrible, and haunts me day and night.'

But Harrowby wrote back in jaunty vein, telling him how unpopular the prospect of peace was with the British public: 'If your terms were yesterday accepted we shall feel that we ought to be more glad than we are. We shall all swing together whenever your signature brings us to the gallows, for nothing but "no peace with Bonaparte" is to be heard from Land's End to Berwick.'

Nobody else seemed to be able to smell death as he could. Cathcart and Stewart might as well have had their nostrils blocked for all the notice they took of their surroundings. His Emperor was not a bad fellow with his long nose and slobbery lower lip, but he would go on talking in his awkward silly fashion about his rights to this or that piffling duchy, and half the time they ought to have been conferring about war and peace they were pinning medals on one another's chests. Well, at least the Emperor had given him a St. Stephen, which made the Russian St. Andrew on Cathcart's chest and the Prussian Black Eagle on Stewart's look tinpot (Wellington was the only other Englishman to have been awarded the St. Stephen).

Sometimes after his megrim cleared, he had a weird feeling of detachment from his fellow human beings. He seemed to be floating not above but amongst them, weightless as a dragonfly. At last Bavaria came over to the Allies, and they outnumbered the French by three to one and, just as the first rains of autumn were beginning to drench the forests of beech and fir, they set off after the French, who were falling back towards Dresden and Leipzig. They trudged on over slushy potholes, living off black bread and potatoes if they were lucky and sleeping where they could.

One night, just after they had crossed the last ridge of Bohemia, George and Metternich, riding together behind the Emperor's party, stopped to let the horses rest, and when they started again, they had lost touch with the others. They blundered on through sleet and soon became aware that they had also lost their way; one muddy track looked much like another in the murk. The track they were on ended at a filthy tumbledown hayloft at the edge of a fir wood. The sleet stopped and they halted to listen for the sound of hooves or carriage wheels. The dripping silence was immense. Then the sky cleared a little, enough to see black clouds assaulting a chill moon.

'It would be foolish to go on, and we are not foolish men, my lord.'

'No, we should bed down here. That would be the prudent thing to do.'

'Let us take refuge in Castle Prudence,' Metternich murmured.

It sounded like advice from *The Pilgrim's Progress*, but George was too tired to ask whether Prince Metternich was acquainted with the works of Bunyan.

They clambered up the old wooden ladder to the loft which had just enough dusty, rat-bitten hay to sleep in. The thin breeze from the wood sighed through the cracks and knotholes in the walls, but the place was dry. They wrapped their greatcoats round them and lay in the dusty straw listening to their horses stirring down below, now and then rubbing along the posts and letting out a tired, shivery snort.

'It is very quiet, is it not? Strange —'

'That over the next hill five hundred thousand men are preparing to kill one another. Yes, and strange too that you and I should be here together. I am not a man for haylofts, I do not think that the Princess Murat would care for this ambience either, although who knows, when she was a little younger perhaps?' He waved a delicate hand at the straw and emitted a reedy chuckle.

'I fear I have not had the pleasure of the Princess Murat's acquaintance.'

'In that, my lord, you are most unusual.'

George was so struck by a man talking of his mistress in this fashion that he could not think what to say. Metternich had no such difficulty.

'Perhaps one should count one's life incomplete if one has not enjoyed a woman in a hayloft, what do you think, my lord?'

'I cannot say. In Scotland the hay would be too damp.'

George was silent, listening to the wind, while

Metternich was busy scrabbling the hay together for his bedding. He moved about the loft on all fours, in the dim light his sly frizzy head like a young rat's. Although he was forty years old, he was so agile, so alert that he made George feel ponderous and old.

'But the way these huge armies are blown towards each other with so little purpose.'

'Ah my lord, I think you are too serious for this game. You must understand that every army, every modern army at least, is propelled by a gigantic afflatus of wind – I mean, of course, public opinion which is splendidly, unflinchingly martial until it is confronted with the cost. And when the winds of war blow, who knows in which direction we shall end up facing?'

'We do, of course, have a cause, we must put an end to Bonaparte's tyranny, and yet every cause must be pursued with a sense of proportion, with . . .' George stopped, uncertain how to proceed and unwilling to seem too portentous at this time of night.

'Proportion!' Prince Metternich blew out his cheeks. The reverberation sounded perilously like a fart. 'War has nothing to do with proportion; on the contrary, by its nature it is excess, frenzy. That is why men like us are so little loved, because we talk about proportion, about balance and bargains instead of glory and destiny. We are the attendants who clean up after the gladiators, we cannot expect garlands.'

'No.'

'We have only the consolation of secretly despising

our masters. But we have to keep the consolation to ourselves, except when we meet our kindred spirits. I am proud to recognise a fellow in you, my lord.'

'I say ditto to that, prince,' George returned with perhaps a smidgeon less enthusiasm.

'And now we must sleep.' Metternich arranged the straw on top of his greatcoat, and closed his eyes almost instantly. But George lay awake half the night, listening to the pluckings and gurglings of their empty bellies. Once or twice, Metternich moved in his sleep and his frizzy head burrowed deeper in the dusty straw and an arm flung out by some nervous spasm clutched at George's greatcoat and the Prince's sly mouth gaping strangely in sleep unleashed a brandy breath which hung in the cold hayloft like a cloud.

'You slept with Prince Metternich . . . in a hayloft?' Stewart liked to play up his deafness and would sidle up to the speaker repeating what he had heard perfectly well, cocking his ear as though proffering a little dish of bonbons.

'In a hayloft, you say.' Cathcart liked to repeat things too, but in a thoughtful manner to suggest that he was deploying superhuman sagacity and squeezing out the last drop of meaning.

'My brother Castlereagh must be informed of this remarkable _démarche_,' Stewart said, choking with laughter.

'Half-brother,' Cathcart added, as he always did.

'Consorting with the agent of a foreign power, eh?'

'But how was it you came to lose touch with us?'

'Lucky you weren't leading a regiment of foot.'

They went on chuckling, and politely George chuckled too but knowing all too well that they would indeed be bombarding Castlereagh with despatches on the subject, putting the most sinister interpretation on his friendship with Metternich.

They galloped on to catch up with their sovereigns, and Aberdeen let his horse plod on at a walk. His only companion now was a surly Austrian dragoon with a face the colour of mouldy cheese. The dragoon had no word of English. The silence was comforting. The only sound was the crunch of their horses' hooves breaking through the thin crust of ice to the foul mud beneath. For the past two days, they had passed through terrible sights, more dead and dying, more smoking rafters and sobbing peasants. The stench had been so disgusting that he was grateful when the homely smell of a manure heap beside a cottage blotted it out and reminded him of Formartine and Methlick.

But now he was alone with the dragoon, riding in a red coat (he did not mind being taken for a soldier) through a defile, bleak and magnificent, with only a few stunted firs clinging to the dark, shiny, splintered rockfaces. The track became narrow and stonier and drier (the water drained off into a black stream alongside the road). The hooves began to chink and ring on the rock. Then the chink and ring seemed to redouble in a laggard echo. There was a sort of rhythm to it, like the slow stamping dances he had seen them do on the little quay beyond the harbourmaster's house in the Piraeus and Catherina had made him try and teased him for his clumsiness. Dum-a-doddly-dum-dum-a-doddy.

The dragoon stopped and turned his horse down towards the stream to let it drink. George stopped too and his reverie was broken. The chinking hooves were silent, but the bass rhythm, that laggard thump, went on, halfway between a boom and a crackle, thunderous. The dragoon unslung his gun and mimicked firing into the air. His cheesy face had a slinky smile on it.

All day George rode under his umbrella to the boom and thump of the guns. For hours, the guns seemed as far away as ever, and then they would turn a bend in the road (the slopes on either side were gentler, now they had come through the pass and were descending into the plain) and the guns would come closer. The sound seemed to bounce off the low bruised clouds and batter at the back of their heads, although it came from twenty miles ahead of them.

In logic it was not surprising that the noise was so terrible. A moment's thought should have prepared George for the likelihood that, sooner or later on this day or the next, he would hear if not witness the greatest bombardment in the history of human warfare. But logical thought could not prepare one for an experience so awesome and so – yes, that had to be said too – so magnificent. It was true what Metternich had said to him in the hayloft, that they were men apart, separated from other people by their loathing of war and waste, by their indifference to military glory, and yet the two of them were as responsible as any other men on earth for arranging this pandemoniac firework display. They had patiently built the alliances, kept the sovereigns from squabbling, brought in the Bavarians, helped to foment the Swiss into rebellion (not an easy people to foment) and fomented the Dutch too, come to that. No men of war could have more subtly and inexorably put together such a herculean display of force than George and his late strawfellow. His stomach felt dull and sick and empty, but somewhere above the foreboding which possessed him (he thought of his brain as those newfangled 'phrenologists' did, with foreboding occupying the lower quarters and the higher segments reserved for lighter activities), he could not help taking note of the ironies and exulting as far as his pride would let him.

A particularly loud bang, and the dragoon growled '*Jawohl!*' and a heavy ape-grin suffused the cheeseface. Why had he been given such a subhuman escort?

The Battle of Leipzig, also known as the Battle of the Nations:

Bonaparte had one hundred and seventy-seven thousand men. He had taken up his headquarters on the slight rise known as Gallows Hill, nailed his map to a farmhouse table in a field of stubble to stop it blowing away, and had a bonfire lit to keep off the October chill.

The Allies had two hundred and fifty-seven thousand men. Bonaparte's plan was first to knock out the Austrians to the south and then turn north to dispose of Blücher's Prussians. Unfortunately, Blücher on this occasion turned up promptly and the French found themselves facing the full Allied force on flat ground where there was no dodging. By the end of the first day, Saturday, after the greatest artillery barrage ever heard (two thousand guns or thereabouts blazing away under the sullen Saxon sky), the French had twenty-six thousand men killed or wounded. On Sunday, they rested, more or less. On Monday, Napoleon's former marshal Bernadotte attacked his old master with sixty thousand Swedes and allsorts. Thousands of Bonaparte's Saxons deserted to the Allies. The Russians came in hard from the south. By Monday evening, the French had lost another twenty thousand men, not to mention the thousands who were drowned in the River Elster after a panicky French corporal had blown up the bridge before all the men were across. The Allies had lost as many men if not more.

George rode in his red coat under his black umbrella across the flat, stubbly battlefield. The next evening, he rode into Leipzig to join his Emperor whose long silly face was flushed with pleasure at his reception.

The townspeople had gone wild with delight. Not one of them, it seemed, had ever huzzaed Bonaparte, nor a single Saxon ever fought for the French intruder. Almost everyone in the Golden Fleece was sozzled. George found Cathcart and Stewart in the snug, writing despatches at a frantic rate with glasses of punch steaming at their side. He looked over Stewart's shoulder: 'The Brandenburg Hussars under my command then proceeded to attack a stoutly held battery to the . . .'

Stewart looked up and said with a smirk: 'Ah, good evening, my lord, I am glad to see you safe and sound. It was a glorious victory, was it not?'

'Glorious, indeed.'

'As a military man, I think I may say with some confidence that when the history of this day comes to be written, the Brandenburg Hussars' attack on Boney's left wing will be regarded as the *coup de grâce*.'

'I'm sure it will.'

Stewart went on smiling his fatuous deaf smile. The victory seemed to have unhinged what was left of his brain.

George went up to his attic room at the top of the hotel. Through the dormer window, he could see out over the roofs of the city to the plain beyond. The smoke of the artillery was still a dark smudge over the plain, the gentler mist of twilight had not yet managed to veil it. He wrote his letter to Maria (he wrote to her every other day if he possibly could).

'How shall I describe the entrance to this town? For three or four miles the ground is covered with bodies of men and horses, many not dead. Wretches wounded, unable to crawl, crying for water amidst heaps of putrefying bodies. Their screams are heard at an immense distance and still ring in my ears. The living as well as the dead are stripped by the barbarian peasantry who have not sufficient charity to put the miserable wretches out of their pain. The whole road to this place is scattered with dead. Single bodies lie at the roadside at such small intervals that we were scarcely a minute or two without repetition of the object; these poor wretches had dropped down from fatigue, some actually in the middle of the road, and the people had not taken the trouble to remove them to the side, although they had all been not only carefully searched for anything of value they might have had, but the bodies were stripped of every vestige of clothing. Our victory is most complete. It must be owned that a victory is a fine thing, but one should be at a distance.'

Out in the street, he heard shouts and singing. The singing sounded raucous, yet strangely tire . He could not even tell in which language the ′ were singing. He looked again at the letter and reviewed in his mind the horrors he had seen. Yet stealing in upon his mind, unasked for, came the thought that he was happy he had chosen to wear a red coat these past days and be taken for a soldier.

Just as he was dropping off to sleep, still sitting up in his rickety wooden chair, there was a knock at the door. George got up and opened it to find to his annoyance the figure of Stewart, rather red in the face and out of breath.

'Upon my life, Aberdeen, this is a queer perch to roost in.'

'The rest of the inn was taken.'

'Well, I thought I ought to let ye have a look at this.' He handed George a document which was already dog-eared and covered with dirt although the paper was fresh enough. It was a despatch from Sir Robert Wilson, his military attaché, dear, dogged, clever Bob Wilson. Desperately scribbled, heat of battle, deafened by cannon fire, and so on. George read on, rather inattentively to start with, expecting stale intelligence of events he had since had a fuller account of. On the contrary, this was a verbatim account of peace proposals from Bonaparte himself, brought back to the Allies by the Austrian general Count Merfeldt who had been taken prisoner and released on parole as an envoy.

'Good heavens, this is tremendous stuff. I'll send a despatch to Lord Castlereagh instantly.'

'Ah well, um, that won't in fact be necessary.'

'Why on earth not?'

'Er, I've already sent a despatch to m'brother, as it happens, in fact. Wilson's ADC bumped into me on the field of battle.'

'But this document is addressed to me,' George said tapping Bob Wilson's spidery handwriting on the cover.

'Yes, yes, so it is. But I thought, you know, to save time, in the interest of the nation –'

'And did you mention the fact that the message was addressed to me?'

'What? Well, no, not in so many words. Time was of the essence. And of course, had you happened to be on the battlefield –'

'Well, then, why didn't you show it to me earlier this evening?'

'Oh, I was writing my report, you know, complicated military matters to expound, slipped my mind, I'm afraid.'

'*Slipped your mind*?' George stared at Stewart's face with intense loathing, imprinted every detail of it in his mind: the fluffy whiskers, the suspicious little pig's eyes, the puffed-up wattles, the mean mouth with the splayed yellow teeth, the general air of umbrageous vanity. Then he took Stewart by his plump little arm and escorted him to the door.

'Goodnight, Sir Charles.'

'Oh what, yes, goodnight then. When my brother comes out here, we'll sort it out, don't you know.'

'Goodnight.'

He wanted to go home now. He had had enough of the smell. He had also had enough of diplomacy in general and more than enough of Cathcart and

Stewart (Sir Charles received the government's thanks and a handsome reward for his brilliance in relaying Bonaparte's peace terms). But he was persuaded to stay on until Castlereagh did come out, and persuaded too to persist until the final terms for peace were negotiated. Not that Castlereagh was under any more illusion than George about how those terms would be received by their fellow countrymen:

> My dear Aberdeen, we must sign. Certainly we must sign. We shall be stoned when we get back to England, but we must sign –
> Yours ever, C.

Home then.

— V —

He came back. He was a
revenant, a sturdy ghost in his rusty black coat,
thicker in the body now and his walk as lumbering as
a farmer's cart, but a ghost all the same. His mind
was distracted, he could not join in the jubilation.
The newspapers were as meaningless to him as if they
were describing the affairs of eskimos or hottentots.
He hugged his dark pale daughters, listened to them
recite the verses they had written to celebrate his
return (his attention sharpened when Jane had to
break off because her cough, that dry hacking cough,
had come back again), smiled at his father-in-law's
gamey anecdotes and talk of poor old Sheridan and
the blowsy royal mistresses and the vulgarity of the
décor at Brighton. But thoughts of death kept
forcing their way back into his mind, and he could

feel his social smile thin upon his face.

The day he came back, he had walked through the lodge gates of Argyll House without warning – the carriage had been stuck in a jam in Piccadilly and he wanted to stretch his legs. The house was shuttered, the front door locked, the bell unanswered. He went round to the tradesman's entrance and found a queer little man in a green apron sawing on a varnished plank.

'It's all shut up. There's floorboards to be made good, and curtains to be hung and I don't know what else.'

'But I sent word from Calais.'

'Ain't no good sending word. There's nobody here. They've all gone to Lord Abercorn's.'

He walked across into Hanover Street and through the quiet streets of Mayfair. The sunshine was gentle and hazy. He felt quite unreal, hollow (well, so he was, he had not eaten since landing soon after midnight), anyone could have walked straight through him.

Outside his father-in-law's house – no it was too much, not after so many months of horror – but he could see from the far side of the square through the trees scarcely out of bud, he could see the streak of pale yellow, the yellow of straw laid to deaden the wheels of the traffic. The door was gaping open at the top of the steps and there in the hall, pacing about, his great red face swollen with tears like a bawling baby, was his father-in-law, much older now, gone in the joints, but not too old to be broken anew by the death of his son and heir.

'Not three days ago, you missed Jamie by three days,' he kept saying. George thought, in the detached otherworldly way which had taken hold of him, so that is what it is like to lose three children in two years; one bawls like a baby and babbles like an idiot.

'Not three days,' Abercorn said once more. 'Ah here's Harriet, ain't she wonderful, ain't she a marvel.'

Down the spiral staircase, heels clicking on the swirling stone steps, her delicate hand gripping the slender railing, came that handsome, sharp-featured young woman whom George had described at Brighton as one of the most stupid persons he had ever met with. How bright her eyes were. She greeted him with a strange fervour which made him feel uncomfortable.

'It is terrible to think of those happy days at Brighton, is it not?'

'Yes, it is.'

'Catherine and her little boy. And now Jamie. Only you and me left to look after so many.'

'Yes, indeed.'

She laid the slender hand upon his forearm, he could feel the tremble of her fingers through the thick black stuff of his coat. He also felt sweat beading upon his brow.

'Ye'll take a chop and a glass of wine, my lord. You have a hungry look about you.'

'Have I? Well, I am hungry. Thank you.' George's voice responded in a mechanical monotone, as though his brain had no part in the speaking.

He sat in the little morning-room with the sun streaming in from the square directly into his eyes and the perspiration pouring off him while he ate.

'Do you mind if I sit with you while you eat?'

'I should be honoured.'

'The truth is, I have scarcely seen a soul save my father-in-law for the past three days and I am devoted to him, but . . .'

'I can imagine.'

'When one is consumed by sorrow, one needs to converse widely, to draw consolation from a variety of sources.'

'I am sure that is wise. I tend to turn in upon myself, I am afraid.'

'You have had much sorrow in your life, have you not? I am less experienced, I fear. I am a poor hand at grieving,' and she began to cry.

He laid his hand upon hers. The sun was now directly opposite the little bow window of the morning-room. He felt unbearably hot in his great travelling-coat. A vast sadness swept over him and made him feel giddy as though he had been rolling down a hill. He could not remember his brother-in-law very well: an amiable fellow, he thought, somewhat alarmed by his father, as who wouldn't be?

Then his daughters came running into the room

and hugged him, and the sadness was bustled out of him.

'Well, well, we'll have to put our heads together to govern this tribe, won't we?' Abercorn had dried his tears for the time being and sat in the wing chair by the fireplace with Harriet's babies crawling over him and George's girls hanging on the arms of the chair.

'I'm as helpless as Laocoön with all these serpents all over me.'

'Oh grandpapa, we aren't serpents.'

'Yes you are.'

'Who's Layoconk?'

'Oh Alice.'

'Your father's the scholar,' Harriet said.

'No longer, I fear.'

Perhaps he wasn't so slow as he felt, because he could read his father-in-law's mind quite effortlessly – not that it really needed reading. George had not been lodged in the house two days before that impulsive old voluptuary declared his thoughts out loud.

'Solitude is a waste of life, you know. In matters of the heart there's nothing to be gained by standing upon ceremony.'

'What? I fear I don't –'

'You're a perfect match. My grandchildren need a father, your girls need a mother.'

'Oh.' George affected to be dumbstruck.

'And besides, it would gladden my black old heart.

Not, of course, that that is a consideration worth a feather.'

'My first thought is always to gratify your wishes, my lord, but –'

'Pish, I know how devoted you were to Catherine, but think about it and don't dawdle. Angels ought to rush in too sometimes.'

He stayed at Bentley until the floorboards had been made good at Argyll House. He had not realised how tired he was. Over the past year, he had ridden across most of Europe, living on black bread and potatoes half the time with the occasional swig of plum brandy. Now he was content to amble through the woods below the Priory. Woods, well, they were little more than thickets of furze and hazel with the occasional birch. The rabbits cropped the grass as close as the nap on velvet, and the six children rolled around the rabbit scrapes and got their petticoats dirty while he and Harriet strolled along behind with the baby Claud wriggling in his nursemaid's arms and greeting the sight of a rabbit sent disappearing into the brambles with a hearty squawk.

He gazed over the huge and gentle panorama: to the right the red roofs and the single spire of Harrow on the Hill, below the Silk Stream just visible through the trees beginning its inconspicuous saunter down to the Thames, the smoky haze of the Great Wen itself, and then beyond, the encircling Surrey hills.

Meanwhile Harriet talked:

'I did not think the dining-room would hold eighteen couple, but Mrs Ratcliffe assures me that indeed it will and that in my late mother-in-law's time they sat down forty to dine with Mr Melville and Mr Pitt and there was plenty of room for the men to serve, but the curtains will need stitching, they are quite frayed at the hems and I'm sure His Lordship would not dream of new ones, wouldn't entertain the notion at all, and I saw such a fine crimson damask in Harris's window, like the curtains in our lodgings at Brighton, only with roses embroidered along the edges. We had fine walks at Brighton, did we not, when we went to see the Pavilion building and that dome like an onion swinging from the ropes all lopsided.' George remembered only the slow waddle of the two dark pregnant women in the rain while he and his brother-in-law shared George's green umbrella. His brother-in-law had not in fact been so very amiable, talked a good deal about the difficulty of extracting rents from his tenantry, and complained of his health, with some reason, it now seemed.

'The Priory is a pleasant spot certainly, but it is too far from Town and yet not far enough. I know that suburban retreats are the fashion now, but I must confess that I prefer one thing or the other. How say you, my lord?'

'I love the Priory,' George answered with feeling.

'Well, of course, I love it too. It's just that I wish it were situated somewhere else. And then, of course, it is small, you know, it's not a house for a family to live in. The nursery wing is decidedly cramped.'

'Perhaps the girls could –'

'No, no, I won't hear of it. Jane and Caroline and Alice must each have their room. And if that means that Claud and little Harriet have to share, we must just put up with it. In any case, I don't want them to be kept awake by the girls' coughing.'

'The coughing is better surely.'

'The coughing is not better. If you had to listen to it every night, my lord, as I do, you would not catch a wink of sleep.'

'I am so sorry.'

'No, it is quite right that you should enjoy a little peace. I declare you look quite restored to your old colour. The Priory is your best medicine.'

And she looked up at him with her dark hooded eyes and her fine sharp lips – she had such an intense look. When she came into his study in the morning (she would often bring him one of her *tisanes* – a lime tea or a glass of peppermint water), he felt as though some beautiful hawk had hopped on to his window-sill. He was alarmed by her as much as he was attracted, yet he found her rattle restful too.

'That piece of plate your brother sent back from Spain is badly discoloured, Tilson took all morning and used a whole jar of Goddard's powder, and still the stain will not shift. And after it cost you twenty pounds to have it sent. That canvas bag was not watertight, I declare it wasn't. Besides, I do not care for an oval dish, I do not know why but I have always had an aversion to oval. He is with the Duke now in the Low Countries, is he not, your brother? A fine-looking man, although a little short in the leg.'

'We are not a long-legged family,' George replied, but he was thinking of his brother Alexander, the flower of all his brothers, brave as a bulldog, ambitious (he had made George scrape acquaintance with poor Lady Wellington at Tunbridge Wells on his behalf), and vain, touchingly vain, always begging George for the price of a fine chased scabbard or a new pair of boots. Alexander had fought side by side with Wellington through every battle in Spain, Portugal and France. The Duke had made him a present of a great black Andalusian horse taken from a dead French officer at Talavera (yet still Alexander described him as 'a man without a *heart*'). George had no cause to complain about Alexander, who had written to him faithfully and regularly, kept him informed of all Wellington's plans (would one call it spying?) and made elaborate arrangements to send captured plate home to Haddo without notifying the authorities (plunder and smuggling?). And now Alexander was riding towards what must be the last encounter with the escaped Bonaparte, and George was walking along the terrace at Bentley with the scent of the wild burnet roses in his nostrils listening to Harriet discourse on the price of renting a house in town and the difficulties her father-in-law was making about her widow's jointure.

'Well, Argyll House will be ready soon,' George said. 'You and the babies may be sure of a welcome there.'

'Oh my lord, *George*,' Harriet said flushing. 'How could you think of such a thing?'

'Ah, you mean . . . But we are under the same roof here, after all.'

'We are under my father-in-law's roof. That is a different matter.'

'I must confess that for my own part I am not much concerned by proprieties of that sort.'

'No doubt, but you are not a widow. We must think of such things, for our children's sake if not for our own.'

'You are quite right, I am sure.' But he was still thinking of his brother Alexander and wondering whether he envied him. It could not be long now before the battle.

Lieutenant-Colonel Sir Alexander Gordon, KCB and holder of the Gold Cross with three clasps for his services at Salamanca, Vitoria, Pyrenees, Nivelle, Alva, Orthes and Toulouse, was wounded on that mournful Belgian plain while arguing with the Duke about the danger his commander was exposing himself to. That night they slept in the same inn at Waterloo. At three in the morning, the Duke's surgeon Dr John Hume, who had cut off Alexander's shattered leg on the battlefield, came to wake his master. The Duke had thrown himself down on his bed, for once too tired to wash. He sat up in bed and stretched out his hand to the doctor. The clasp was as firm as ever. With head lowered, Dr Hume said that Alexander had just died in his arms. He felt tears dropping on his hand, then he raised his head and saw tears on the Duke's face making furrows in the sweat and grime.

'Well, thank God, I don't know what it is to lose a battle, but certainly nothing can be more painful than to gain one with the loss of so many of one's friends.'

The Duke wrote a fine poignant letter to George and in a postscript said he would keep Alexander's horse 'till I hear from you what you wish should be done with it'. That rosy-cheeked Scotsman whom George had first met acting in *The Rivals* at Bentley wrote a poem, *The Field of Waterloo*, not one of his finest – his sinews were a little too stiff for verse by this time – in which the reader was conducted around the battlefield and enabled to see 'generous Gordon, 'mid the strife fall while he watch'd his leader's life'. And so he had.

For the rest of his life, George cherished the Duke's letter and a copy of Sir Walter's poem, and they raised a memorial on the mournful plain (the only British memorial there, as it happened): 'In testimony of feelings which no language can express, a disconsolate sister and five surviving brothers have erected this simple memorial to the object of their tenderest affection.' They built a replica at Haddo too. It had been intended they should all contribute to the expense, but Charles and John were seldom in funds and elusive even when they were (indeed, had Alexander himself been one of those expected to contribute to such a memorial, it is doubtful whether he would have stumped up). In the event though, it turned out that Alexander had made himself so agreeable in Brussels that the principal citizens were only too happy to bear the cost.

The night after the tired messenger had ridden up the gravel at Bentley and been entertained to mutton broth in the servants' hall, George sat in his bedroom writing letters to be dispatched in the morning, to his other brothers and his sister Alicia and to others who had known and loved Alexander.

There was a light tread in the passage outside, the doorhandle was twisted open by a practised hand and there in the dim light stood Harriet with her hair down and a long silk dressing-gown of jade green, a somewhat sickly colour, he remembered thinking when she had first worn it to breakfast.

'My lord, I could not sleep for thinking of your sorrow.' She held out her hands to him, and he took them with a lack of hesitation in which he surprised himself. The kiss which followed had no mourning delicacy about it. Even in the first embrace, he could not help noticing how tightly she held him. He could not remember a woman holding him so tightly before, certainly not either of the Catherines. They went hand in hand towards the bed with a trancelike propulsion and then he stopped thinking and gave himself over to unrestrained passion. Only in the final moments did his consciousness free itself again and hover above him like an engineer overseeing a great steam engine. By God, she gripped him tight, he thought they would never end, and when they collapsed, two wet shuddering animals on the old pink counterpane, he felt there was nothing left of him.

They were married a month later at Stanmore in the crumbling rose-brick church below the hill. As he looked up during the parson's homily, George saw weeds growing in the angles of the sagging rafters. The jackdaws in the roofless tower cawed throughout the service and were only frightened away by the bells at the end when George and Harriet came down the aisle past the small congregation who looked respect-ful rather than joyful, he thought. The *Middlesex Gazette* described Harriet as a radiant Waterloo bride, which was truer than the *Middlesex Gazette* could know. It was a day of rejoicing all round, 8 July. Louis XVIII entered into Paris, to become the third ruler of France in three weeks. Napoleon had abdicated in favour of the poor King of Rome just after Waterloo and sailed for Plymouth on the *Bellerophon* the day of the wedding. Hearing the news as they bobbed along in the carriage away from the church, George had a gay fancy that Bonaparte had been trying to come to their wedding. He pictured the stunned Stanmore congregation as that liverish figure, less slight now and the eye less bright no doubt than at Malmaison, stumped up the aisle to take the pew of honour on the groom's side. He tried to convey this phantasm to his bride, but Harriet was irritated rather than amused, then repenting, clasped his hand in her fierce grip.

But there was no getting away from it, Harriet was easily irritated and not easily amused. In London, she complained of the dust and the mephitic odours of Soho. She would like to lift up Argyll House and transplant it a mile to the West in the purer air of Mayfair. It was not a good place for Jamie and Claud and little Harriet to grow up in. He took her north to Haddo to view his improvements: the splendid lake which had replaced the snipe-marsh in front of the house, the spanking roads which had replaced the muddy rutted tracks, the terraces, the flowerbeds. There was even a hothouse which had cost him two thousand pounds. Above all, there were trees: the grand avenue, a mile long from the house to the eastern horizon, the plantations beyond and the hanging woods full of the pheasants he had put down. And the smiling tenantry with their roofs repaired, their fences made good – why, it was as good as living in Hampshire. But not to Harriet. She took days to recover from the six days of bumping about in a carriage to get there, and her spirits never really recovered. Oh the north, she would say with a shiver as she came down into the morning-room, is that the Arctic Circle I see out of the window? A letter from a friend who had been frequenting the new Assembly Rooms at Brighton threw her into a sulk which lasted all day.

By the next summer, she was pregnant and had an excuse to go to Brighton herself and take all the children with her, on the grounds that southern sea air would be as good for their delicate chests as the northern blasts were harmful. George went north and planted trees for eight hours a day with only one or two of his remaining bachelor brothers, John, Charles and William, for company; John and William fell asleep after dinner every night; William snored; Charles went up to his bedroom and played his flute interminably. They all drank a good deal of their brother's wine. George himself drank almost nothing and lived on a cold partridge for breakfast and a hot one for dinner at six-thirty. He spent the evening writing long letters to Harriet telling her that her aches and pains were of no great consequence.

Plunging through the sedgy marshes after duck and snipe, he could forget how lonely he was and how anxious for one or other of his children. In the stubblefields of September, he was remorseless after partridge, eager to pursue the most elusive covey over hedge and ditch. Walking twenty miles a day until his calves felt as though they had red-hot irons in them –

that was his extremity of pleasure. In other people's houses, too, exhaustion made rural society tolerable in the evenings: he would doze lightly as the lady of the house tried to amuse him, or some local archdeacon, imported to cater to his supposed interest in ecclesiastical matters (he had very little beyond the call of duty, as it happened), would become heated on the danger of the High-Church enthusiasm. He would mumble apology, he feared he was not up in the subject, being a somewhat lapsed Presbyterian.

When the ground was frozen hard and there was no sport, he would sit in his room and try to read Racine but instead begin fretting about his wife's health or one of the children's, and feel guilty that he was not with them. When he came down to dine, he would be edgy and morose and even the most enchanting woman would find him hard going. But there was one exception. He would always light up when the Russian ambassadress was standing there among the ladies with her long nose and sharp eyes questing about the room. Madame de Lieven, Princesse de Lieven, had been, perhaps still was, the mistress of Metternich and who knew how many other statesmen – Canning, Castlereagh, even the Duke himself? There was no great man living whom she had not swept up – so long as the great man was dedicated to the preservation or restoration of the *ancien régime*. She collected them like works of art, but she had her principle of selection, like a connoisseur whose

cupidity seems boundless but is in fact strictly confined to altarpieces of the Bolognese school. *La
bécassine* she was called by her numerous detractors,
and indeed there was something snipelike not just
about her long nose and close-set eyes but about her
way of darting across a room and about the flight of
her conversation too – urgent yet at the same time
erratic and without apparent destination. You never
knew where she was going or where she would end
up. She wanted to know everything: what the Duke
really thought of Peel, what Peel really thought about
the Catholics, was Lord Palmerston really the lover of
Lady Sarah?

'He is said to prefer Lady Eliza.'

'But my lord, you are quite out of date. That was
last season. You might as well be dwelling in
Timbuctoo.'

'Madam, I do live much out of the world.'

'Nonsense, everyone says you are the best-
informed man in London.'

'Everyone is mistaken, madam. I am at most one of
the best-informed men in north Aberdeenshire.'

'On the contrary, when we last met in Tunbridge
Wells you were a fountain of information. And what
do you think of that absurd creature Metternich? Is he
not a ruined man, ruined by his vanity and
inconstancy?'

'Absurd, madam? You know I count him as one of
my oldest friends, I had thought that you too . . .'

'My lord, you see I was right, you listen to gossip, but *very old* gossip. You probably have not seen Prince Metternich for years.'

'That is true, alas.'

'He has gone down the hill. He has become a bore, he will not stop talking, he is what you call a rattle. Can a man be a rattle? At all events, he is certainly an idiot. Can you conceive anything more foolish than his new marriage – to a stupid girl half his age and without a penny or a quartering to her name.'

He liked the way *la bécassine* cocked her head on one side to consider the effect of what she had said before darting off again. Did he know that Mr Canning said he had been in love with her for thirteen years, but never dared tell her so, he had once taken her into his bedroom and showed her a little sketch of her by Lawrence which he had just bought and said Heaven had made them for each other. What did Lord Aberdeen think of that?

'Canning was a great man.'

'Very possibly, but an insincere lover. He always shut his eyes when I was talking to him. I never believed a word he said to me.'

'I shall remember always to keep my eyes open when I have the honour to be in your company.'

When he met Harriet again in London, their long-distance misunderstandings were forgotten. They went at each other with the same impatient ferocity. When he had recovered his breath, George sometimes thought that there was not much love in it, and wondered whether she thought the same but knew enough to see that there was no way of asking her.

And in any case, his doubts were swallowed up – or postponed anyway – by the arrival of his son and heir George, and then a year later Alexander (after the fallen hero) and the year after that a daughter Frances. Three in three years, just like Catherine. Now there were nine of them, the strain of that would tell on the saintliest of women, even on – no he must not think like that, he must not make comparisons, he must take Harriet as she was and he *had* taken her. And she was a handsome and spirited creature, never more in bloom than when she was with child, only –

But there came a time when she was not with child and when even little Frances had a nursemaid looking after her and then the fact had to be faced. Three of the blessed brood of nine – the nine muses, the nine worthies, the nine bright shiners – were not hers, and she made it painfully, acidly clear that they weren't.

It was not that she was without compassion or sympathy. When Caro first became ill at Argyll House, Harriet urged her two sisters who were up at the Priory to write to her every day by 'the cart', the rumbling old carrier's vehicle which took fruit and vegetables and fresh linen down to Argyll House. And when Jane (who liked to know things properly) asked her whether Caro would ever get better, she wrote back at length.

'As to what you ask me my dear Jane about poor Caro – it is difficult for me to answer you – you know that all things are possible to God – and that if it is his will he may still permit her to recover even after this lingering and dangerous illness – but the probabilities I am forced to say appear against it – for her weakness is so great. But I must earnestly beg you not to dwell upon the subject more than you can help – for two reasons – that whatever God orders is for the best tho' we cannot see why – and that the thing that would make Papa and me more unhappy under this misfortune would be seeing you both ill and unhappy. Bless you my dearest Jane.'

That was certainly a straight enough answer, and a true prognosis, for Caro had tuberculosis of the spine and died, a sad shrunk little scrap of a person, in the summer of 1818, her tenth. Caro's death brought all George's old grief flooding back, as if it had been merely pent in a sullen millpond waiting for the clank of the sluice-gates. But the sight of his tearstained monkey face had a terrible effect on his wife. Her jealousy had been pent up too – the jealousy of a first wife who was supposed to have been more perfect than any other human being and whom she only remembered as a jolly pregnant fellow-waddler along the Steyne at Brighton. Now there was another ghost in the house and Harriet became irritable to the point of hysteria. She hated the letters George wrote her telling her to pull herself together: 'I do not like the thought of your being so low and nervous, especially as you have no good reason. Patience is difficult but I feel satisfied that is all that is required.' He had the graceless habit of going on to discuss his own headaches and shooting pains and then the rest of his letter would be devoted to instructions for looking after the children, especially Jane and Alice with their bad throats and their high fevers. Instructions from Haddo, instructions from Woburn Abbey, from the Ashburnhams in Sussex where he had been shooting and from the Bathursts in Cirencester. And what was he doing the long country evenings after he had pulled off his muddy topboots and his man had brought him a basin to soak his swollen feet in and he came downstairs spruced up or as spruce as he could be bothered in his shabby old frock coat? Who did he glimpse at the end of the long gallery with her snipe's face and sharp snipe's eyes raised to see who had come through the double doors? No doubt Princess Lieven had agitated to make sure of coinciding with him, for she was an indefatigable agitator, but he did not mind that. There was no one on earth he would rather gossip with, no one who was so light on her pins and whirled him in a conversation so quick and gossamer that they might have been mayflies instead of middle-aged persons. They found more and more in common, above all, an ever growing detestation of Cupid – *'J'aime mieux les rouges que Lord Palmerston,'* she would break out – and that was saying something, for *la bécassine*'s hatred of

Jacobins made George himself feel deliciously radical. And then one evening, in a great Sussex house, in the little brown saloon with the Turner sketches, she let her long bony hand play over his stubby paw, scarcely touching the tips of his fingers with hers.

'*Ce soir*, my lord . . .?'

He was lonely that evening, and sore with the world. There was a dark hallway where she turned off the upper passage to go to her room and there for a moment she paused, seeming to look for something in her reticule, a lanky ghost in the darkness. And he too turned out of the passage and took her in his arms and kissed her fiercely.

Too fiercely. His teeth rattled against hers. She was startled, uttered a faint cry, a cry she had not intended, would not have uttered if the breath had not been knocked out of her body. In that brief moment he held her, he was aware of an odd smell about her, a faint fishy odour behind her cologne. But it was only a brief moment. The faint cry was enough to frighten him off. He leapt a pace backward, muttered something, he did not know what, and turned back in the passage.

The incident was never mentioned again. Far from ruffling their friendship, they were firmer friends than ever, commiserated over bereavements and illnesses and disappointments, rejoiced in occasional windfalls, and groaned at human folly in general and the idiocy of modern politicians in particular. They corresponded for twenty years until an event which both of them had dreaded and fought against broke their friendship for ever. But all the time he could never quite get the fishy smell out of his mind.

Meanwhile, there was Harriet, barely able to move with eight sickly children and two ghosts on her hands, and him looking so grave and impeccable and irreproachable. It was enough to make a person spit, and spit she did.

Jane was the target. Alice was already too ill, the doctors could no longer conceal their fear that she too might have pulmonary tuberculosis. Like her mother, they bled her as often as they dared, they dosed her with chloride of mercury, they sealed the windows of her bedroom so that no draughts could enter. Amazingly, Alice survived and even seemed to get better. Meanwhile, Jane had recovered from the aphthae in her throat and looked robust enough. She had a natural self-confidence which gave life to the monkey face she had inherited from her father. Everyone loved her. She was as bright a fifteen-year-old as could be imagined. Her only failing was that she was boisterous, and now and then made her little Hamilton cousins cry.

It was the sound of Claud wailing along the nursery corridor that provoked Harriet's first outburst. Jane was a bully, a monster, an unnatural child, her father must come straight home and deal with her, she had never seen such a child, she had been allowed to run wild, Mrs Gale had been quite unqualified as a nurse, there was in any case irrefutable evidence that Mrs Gale drank.

Lord Aberdeen read this letter as he was chewing on a kidney in Lord Bathurst's morning-room and nearly choked on it. He had never received such an abusive and vengeful letter, certainly not from a woman and not, of course, from (but clearly he must not think of her). The letters which followed (literally followed him on his stately progress around the country) coupled abuse of Jane with abuse of him, for his callousness, his neglect, his utter indifference to any other human being, especially to his wretched wife, if wife he still called her.

He wrote back: 'You ask if I think of you when I go to bed in our room. I have told you dearest that I always do. I think that if I were sure of finding you there tonight I should go with about a thousand times more pleasure.'

And then in the next letter, she would return to the subject of Jane: 'If I should die, I insist that Jane shall not have charge of my children, for she will mistreat them and neglect them so that they were better off in the orphanage. You must draw up a legal document to protect my children and our children too.' She covered several more pages in the same vein.

He wrote back bewildered, trying to understand, but fatally unable to conceal his resentment. 'The whole is so strange and unaccountable that when I view the thing deliberately I can scarcely think it possible. My whole wish and desire are confined to one word – "Be kind". If you answer in substance, "I hate your child, and therefore I cannot be kind," you must not be surprised if I am not quite satisfied. What I have to complain of is the declared and avowed hatred of a stepmother. Now when I married you, although I certainly had no right to expect that my children would meet with equal love, yet I had good reason to suppose that they would never be regarded *with indignation and disgust.*' When he underlined the last phrase, he found that his hand was shaking.

He sent her partridges, he spoke again of the joy of holding her in his arms: 'As you like to hear it, and in the hope that it will make up for other matters, I will tell you, most dear and sweet love, I love you most ardently and long to kiss and embrace you ten thousand times.' She snorted (her long nostrils flared like a horse's). The plodding transparent falsity of these phrases would not divert her from her insistence that Jane should be legally barred from the guardianship of her children. He groaned, pulled off his muddy boots (he had been shooting snipe in the marsh beyond the new plantation at Formartine) and wrote back promising that a deed should be formally executed as she wished. He finished: 'And now, my love, if my fate should be that which you have anticipated for yourself, how am I to diminish its bitterness? To whom am I to look, and what promise can I exact? Alas! I can only trust that my death may soften the cruelty of those feelings which have hitherto been proof against every other consideration.'

The promise was not put to the test. Despite the swollen glands in her neck and the terrible cough, Jane began to go out by herself – to the opera, to dine at Lady Wicklow's, to a concert at Lady Melville's, writing always to their beloved Mrs Gale, to keep her up with the news. On one such letter, there is a note in pencil (Mrs Gale's hand probably): *'Lady Jane went to the Priory as here proposed and the next week expired after two days illness the greater part of which she was in convulsions. How caused it was never ascertained. She died July 1824 anno aetatis 18.'*

He was determined at least, at last, to save Alice. For a time too, he thought Harriet might help him. Some nobler part of her nature would understand that he must keep alive the only relic of Catherine, the last sweet trembling reminder of perfection. When he said that Alice must not spend another winter in England, Harriet agreed and he was delighted. When he spoke of taking a house in Nice, she said it would be most agreeable to spend a month or two there. George wrote that day to an agent who secured them a villa for six months at a hundred and fifty louis a week, including plate, linen and crockery.

But when he set off in December with Alice, Harriet said she would follow later. She had begun making difficulties and describing the whole trip as an infernal bore. She also seemed to have lost interest in Alice's coughs and swellings, even in the slight lameness which had come on lately and seemed to be getting worse. George began to see that it was only the unexpectedness of Jane's death that had temporarily changed her.

He was glad to be on his way. Alice was such a winning companion. For all her ill health, she had the same sense of humour, the same quick eye as her mother. When they were walking among the pink and white chrysanthemums at the Tuileries, she was the first to notice how the royal initials effaced during the revolution had been restored on the façade, the Ls back in place where the Ns and the bees had been only a few years earlier. In Lyons, when George ordered sal volatile to restore her, she instantly spotted that the apothecary thought he intended to drink the stuff, having heard fearsome stories of the English capacity for spirits. And when they found themselves at last walking on the high path looking out over the orange roofs and the palm trees to a sea bluer and brighter than she had seen, her happiness pierced him to the heart so that he had to keep back his tears.

They would wander (slowly for she was weak but a good distance because she was determined) along the scented paths behind the villa, botanising and practising their French to one another, making up absurd names for the flowers they could not identify. George felt his own strained health begin to improve in step with Alice's.

When Harriet arrived after Christmas with an exhausted army of servants and several coachloads of baggage, the fragrant peace of the villa was broken in an instant.

'I must say you seem to have settled in here like an old married couple. Alice, where did you get that costume?'

'Papa bought it for me, in the Rue Sainte-Hélène.'

'Well, it may do very well in the Rue Sainte-Hélène, but I don't think it's the thing for an English miss. Uncle John and Uncle Charles will be struck dumb to see you wearing such a thing.'

George saw his bachelor brothers giving conflicting instructions about the luggage. In their tight English coats and their imposing whiskers, they brought instant gloom to the light and airy Maison Avigdor. The botanising walks continued, but now they seemed furtive and constrained. In the clear air, they could sometimes hear Harriet talking to John or Charles on the terrace several hundred yards below. The house seemed full of servants. The bachelor brothers dozed on the terrace or disappeared into the town on long excursions about which they had little to say on their return. Harriet insisted on engaging a music master for Alice, and the noise of her practising made the Maison Avigdor seem surprisingly small. The bases of the big blue Sèvres vases on the commode were uneven. Alice's high notes made them vibrate with a little impatient drumming sound.

'The isle is full of noises and a thousand twangling instruments hum about mine ears.'

'You know how I dislike quotations. We must not interrupt her practising. I had hoped you would have engaged Monsieur Fumaroli before I arrived.'

'He was not at liberty. In any case, Alice needed time to enjoy Nice first.'

'I dare say, but I sometimes wonder whether a little hard work may not be the best remedy for her. She needs to be distracted from her ailments.'

'My dear, her ailments are very real. I do not see how she may easily be distracted from them.'

'Children often exaggerate, you know. I have noticed, for example, that she coughs very seldom when she is practising.'

'*Exaggerate.*' But he reflected, just in time, how much trouble he had finally had in persuading Harriet to come to Nice and how much trouble he would have if she went home again, and so he ended limply: 'I really don't think she does exaggerate, my dear.'

'Fathers are the last to see. But let us say no more on the subject. Have you noticed how much your brothers drink? Mr Grant informs me that he has had to send out for another dozen of claret.'

'Harriet, they are *en vacances*. In any case, it was you who brought them out here, though of course I am heartily glad to see them.'

'I do not want military habits imported into my household. Perhaps you could say something to them, or to Charles at any rate, he is the more reasonable of the two.'

'I certainly could not. You do not seem to understand how delicate is the situation of an elder brother. I have had charge of their finances ever since they were boys. Surely you must see how they would resent advice on such a subject.'

'I see only that I have a right to expect certain standards to be maintained in my household. I have no objection to wine in moderation, certainly not in France, but I will not see my house turned into a barracks.'

Altogether it was a relief the following winter when Harriet decided, definitively this time, not to come with them. Alice was measurably worse that winter. Much of the time she had a fever and swellings in her neck and legs which the doctors feared were a sign of heart trouble. Perhaps she might improve with better weather.

He began to place desperate trust in the spring. The first buds of almond blossom and mimosa in their walks above the villa produced an absurd rush of hope in him. He felt the warmth of the sun on his back and could not help believing that it would heal Alice too.

But at the same time he had to shut his mind to Harriet's letters. Remorseless and regular they came, full of complaints about her stomach, her nerves, her agitation of mind, his neglect, his callousness, his indifference. Any proper husband would never have left her in such a condition, any proper husband would rush back to her side, realising his error. He wrote back alternately soothing, baffled, indignant, but finally apologetic, grovelling, lying: 'The pain of separation which I experienced in leaving you was a hundred times greater than I shall feel in leaving her. I cannot conceal from myself that she is in a helpless situation. It is true I may have lamented the impossibility of uniting two things perfectly incompatible, viz. the power of being in two places at once.' But the hesitation had been only momentary. He had to go to Harriet.

And so he left Alice, in a strange country, without friend or relative, only Miss Holloway her governess, and posted to Paris, stopping neither to dine nor sleep, eating a cold fowl in the carriage when he was hungry. In Paris he stopped to buy Harriet some white dinner plates as she did not like his blue Staffordshire ones.

Alice survived that winter and the one after that and the one after that, just. But by the following spring, she was very weak. On 29 April 1829, she died in her father's arms (she had lain there for hours previously).

He went to the Foreign Office and shut himself up there for four days absolutely alone. His grief was terrible. It was not true for him that after the first death there was no other.

It is worth noting, but only now, that Lord Aberdeen had become Foreign Secretary the preceding spring.

And what did he achieve? Ah, that is a brutal question to ask of any statesman, one usually wearily addressed after pages of tortuous narrative, spiced with lumbering anecdote and cautious character assessment, but with George, almost unique among Foreign Secretaries of the nineteenth or any other century, the whole point is to cut all that and go straight to the bottom line.

First of all, he persuaded the Duke not to issue an ultimatum if the French sent a fleet to the Peloponnese. There was no war between Britain and France or between France and the Turks and the Egyptians, or between Britain and the Turks. Against considerable opposition, he raised the Allied blockade of Crete. Against even greater opposition, including that of his own brother Robert (whom he had sent to succeed Stratford Canning at Constantinople), he refused to allow the British fleet to advance to defend the entry to the Bosphorus from the Russians. The world held its breath. Would the Russians advance to take Constantinople? They did not, they halted, they signed the Peace of Adrianople with the Turks, much on the terms that their Foreign Minister Nesselrode (remembered for the pudding that was named after him) had outlined a couple of months earlier to Aberdeen's man at the Russian headquarters in Odessa. The Duke made Aberdeen send off a fiery despatch condemning the terms of the Treaty, but in practice the outcome could have been worse: the

Sultan propped up for another decade or two, peace on the border between Russia and Turkey, the creation of an independent Greek state – a sentimental dream of George's, though not of the Duke's.

During the same period in office, George and the Duke between them managed not to intervene to support Donna Maria and her constitutionalist party in the quarrel over the succession to the Portuguese throne – despite thunderous attacks from Lord Palmerston, or 'Pam', as Cupid was now known. Cupid was equally hot for the right of Donna Isabella and *her* constitutionalists to the Spanish throne. How splendidly he denounced the pretensions of the wicked uncles in both countries. George, on the whole, took the view that there was nothing much more to be said for one side than the other. He did not believe in Cupid's preference 'for intermeddling, intermeddling in every way and to every extent short of actual military force'. And before he and the Duke were turfed out, George kept Britain out of two more imbroglios: the revolution of 1830 which brought Louis-Philippe to the French throne (he had a struggle to persuade the Duke to recognise the bourgeois monarch, but he succeeded) and the other revolution which split Belgium off from Holland, which he himself was reluctant to accept because he believed in maintaining existing boundaries. Cupid took the credit for the eventual birth of Belgium as a consequence of the interminable London conference, but it was George who had presided over its early sessions and set its course.

What else? He threatened Spain when there were rumours of a Spanish expedition from Cuba to regain Mexico. No expedition was sent. And there was trouble in South America too. The government in Buenos Aires declared Louis Vernet governor of the Malvinas Islands. George protested. A couple of years later, Palmerston sent a naval detachment. Buenos Aires protested. George, back again as Colonial Secretary, was unpersuaded that the Falkland Islands, as we called them, would be as important for the Pacific trade as the Cape of Good Hope was for the Indian trade. The question whether to go on occupying the islands was still unsettled when George retired. Cupid, himself back in office again, settled it by sending out two or three fishermen from the Orkney and Shetland Islands who were used to high winds and an absence of trees.

But we are jumping ahead of ourselves. The score must be kept. In George's first spell at the Foreign Office, Britain had used the threat of force several times but had in the event kept out of at least eight furious international disputes. Not a drop of British blood had been spilled, except for two sailors who had been killed in a brawl in Plymouth by some Portuguese refugees who had been behaving badly. British power and prestige had seldom stood higher. Not bad for a man who seemed drained by grief and appeared to walk through life sunk in the sombre.

Next, he was Colonial Secretary for a year. His first task was to implement the abolition of slavery throughout the dominions (his first vote in Parliament had been given for the abolition of the slave trade). He overcame the difficulties in Jamaica. He issued instructions for the humane treatment of the kafirs in the Cape and the Griquas up on the Orange River. He began to formulate a constitutional settlement for Canada which looked remarkably like the one Lord Durham came up with three years later. But by that time Peel was out, and so was he. During his year at the Colonial Office his grief had no cause to dry up. The year before, Harriet had taken the hypochondriac's revenge and died – from tuberculosis, like Caro and Jane and Alice. He wrote from Haddo to his eldest son, now aged seventeen: 'The gloom and desolation of the place, under present circumstance, can scarcely be endured. No sunshine or fine weather, either in winter or summer, can ever make amends for the loss of that perpetual sunshine within. I shall go on with all the projected improvement and alterations, for your sake at least, as any pleasure which I can now receive from what is done will be but small.' The difference in the mourning is painful to see: the first time, there had been bright vital agony – the snapping of a green stick – now there was only sullen despair, the dull crunch underfoot of a rotten bough. A few months later, his last daughter Frances caught cold at the Priory and died at the age of sixteen. The nine bright shiners were down to five (although they had had two more sons later on, Douglas and Arthur: even at the worst that hard, impatient impulse had never left either of them).

But here we must pause and reckon with a different kind of stress. For as we go on, the more we must admit, uneasily, shifting in our seats, that this is not a narrative for modern readers. There is something off-putting, even repellent, about George's refusal to be made useless by his grief. So far as we know, he utters no senseless cry, permits himself no futile gesture. Let us try our best for him: maddened by grief, he buries himself in work, his dispatches have a frantic keening note which bewilders their recipients, his wild eye, his bouts of distraction become an embarrassment. Unfortunately, none of this is true. It is noticed that he has grown a little grubby in his dress (and even that is mostly because he is so frequently in motion between his far-flung homes and his laundry never catches up with him). Otherwise, the good-humoured moderation of his speech and writing is unimpaired. He even learns to speak a little louder in the House of Lords.

And he becomes Foreign Secretary for another five years, under Peel. He settles the baleful and seemingly insoluble quarrels with France (and, by the way, it is he, not Edward VII sixty years later, who mints the phrase 'Entente Cordiale'). He avoids another war over Greece. He insists on reaching a settlement of the wars with China and secures Hong Kong for the Crown. With his friend Guizot he settles the ludicrous but menacing affair of the Spanish marriages. He settles two bitter boundary disputes with America, over Maine and Oregon (Cupid excelled himself in abuse over the Maine treaty). Within living memory, Britain had gone to war with both France and America, and public opinion on both sides was eager for a replay. Any one of these questions might have led to ruinous and futile bloodshed. The settlement of them led to nothing but increased trade, prosperity and co-operation.

Across the rest of Europe revolutions came and revolutions went, but the peace of Europe was preserved and England was a haven still for all those whose own countries had become too hot to hold them. From Brighton, Princess Lieven with her last lover, none other than Monsieur Guizot, lately the Prime Minister of France, wrote to say that she was bored of having to see Metternich every day with his fat, vulgar third wife. He had become so intolerable, never stopped talking, still full of his own infallibility (why then had he finished up in lodgings in Brighton?), charming only when he talked about the past and above all about Napoleon. George thought fondly, sadly, of the three elderly exiles stumping along the promenade where he and both his wives had strolled nearly forty years before: Guizot and the Princess both terrified of the damp and so muffled up that they would catch only one word in three of Prince

Metternich's interminable monologue whistling through the autumn wind. The ex-Russian Ambassadress, the ex-Minister of Austria, the ex-Prime Minister of Louis Philippe – a sad parody of those gay glittering conclaves of Teplitz and Vienna. The congress no longer danced, it hobbled, and towards the exit.

What was his policy? The way he put it himself (and who else was to blow that particular trumpet?) was that 'It has been marked by a respect due to all independent States, a desire to abstain as much as possible from the internal affairs of other countries, an assertion of our own honour and interests, and, above all, an earnest desire to secure the general peace of Europe by all such means as were practicable and at our disposal.' In and out of public office over forty years or so, he had first helped to settle the peace in Europe, then helped to keep it despite Cupid rattling his bow and arrow whenever he was in and George was out. Surely therefore he had a right to expect – no, no, what a peculiar thought to embark on. You fail to understand entirely. People don't read history to be grateful, and historians don't write it to say thank you. Anyway historians tend to be peppery characters who like to see action, at the safe distance of a century or so. Like the rest of us they want to be amused and taken out of themselves. Alas, the language of moderation, of balance, worse still of judgement, has an irremediable staleness. The longer and deeper the historian delves into the archives, the more greedily he pounces on a bright phrase, a bold gesture, a dashing *démarche*. So: who remembers George, or the forty years of peace? If only he had cut his throat like Castlereagh, now that would be a different matter.

'Then there is the matter of this Jew, my lord.'

'Which Jew?'

'A Portuguese Jew by the name of David Pacifico. He styles himself Don Pacifico or *le chevalier* Pacifico, although his character gives him small claim to either title. He was ejected from Portugal in dubious circumstances, many years ago. The captain of an English vessel, the *Berwick Packet*, sold his ship because he could not defray the cost of repairs, and was paid in a forged bill by the same Pacifico, who decamped to Morocco where he became Portuguese consul and then later to Greece where he performed the same office until he was dismissed seven or eight years ago. The complaints against him had become intolerably numerous. He has continued at Athens as a moneylender to the indulgent citizens of that city.'

'Well, well, and —'

'You may remember from your Greek travels, my lord, that each year on Easter Sunday the Athenian mob takes great delight in burning an effigy of Judas Iscariot.'

'I never saw the ceremony, but I heard tell of it.'

'Well, on Easter Sunday Baron de Rothschild was present in Athens to discuss the repayment of his loan. The Greek government was naturally eager to endear itself to that gentleman, so the Greek police took measures to prevent the people from assembling for the bonfire. A rumour circulated in the neighbourhood that it was Pacifico who had obtained the ban, so they attacked and burnt his house instead and either plundered or destroyed every stick of furniture in it.'

'Poor fellow. But what has this to do with us? My concern for the fate of Greece is considerable but I cannot see that the maltreatment of a former Portuguese consul, deplorable though it may have been, is a matter which —'

'Pacifico was born in Gibraltar.'

'Was he, dammit?'

'He has recently taken out a British passport.'

'And thrown himself on Lord Palmerston's mercy?'

'Precisely so, my lord.'

'Thank heavens I'm no longer at the Foreign Office.'

'Lord Palmerston has taken up the case. He takes a strong view of the matter.'

'He always takes a strong view of the matter. On second thoughts, perhaps it would be better if I were still at the Foreign Office.'

Even so, it did not enter his head that the affair could not be settled in the usual way of such things.

'The Pacifico business, my lord.'

'Not again surely. It is two years, no, more.'

'Nearer three, my lord. Since Admiral Parker happens to be in the Eastern Mediterranean, Lord Palmerston has taken the opportunity to instruct him to drop anchor off the Piraeus and instruct the Greek Foreign Minister that unless his government pays the full compensation to Pacifico within twenty-four hours, he will take action against Greek shipping. The seizure of Greek merchant ships is not excluded.'

'And at what do the demands of our esteemed fellow-countryman stand?'

'Thirty-one thousand pounds. That is his claim on the Greek government. He has also outstanding claims on the Portuguese government of some twenty-one thousand pounds for lost documents and services rendered, although the Portuguese say they don't owe him a shilling.'

'Thirty-one thousand pounds for a few broken chairs and cups and saucers. He must have been in a very prosperous way of business.'

'On the contrary, my lord. I understand he was rather poor.'

'Why has he still not tried the Greek courts?'

'He prefers to throw himself upon the mercy of his Queen.'

'I must have seen Pam at work at least for thirty years but I still find him hard to credit. To send a fleet more powerful than that which won the Battle of the Nile, and to threaten a friendly country, one which we have established and nursed not a dozen years past, and all for . . . *le chevalier* Pacifico.'

'You remember there are other matters in contention, my lord: the alleged torture of Stellio Sumachi, for example, and the case of HMS *Fantome*. While you were in Scotland, Blue Books have been prepared setting out the matters at issue. Lord Stanley is talking of a motion of censure.'

'I shall be happy to speak to it when the time comes.'

Even now, in his sixties, he felt the old tremble at the prospect of battle, the zinging sensation in his head, the lurch in his stomach. This time, surely, Cupid could be trounced. His behaviour had been so absurdly out of proportion, his umbrage so childish, everyone must see at last how utterly unfit he was for that office which he swaggered about in like a prizefighter in a fairground.

And Stanley was the man to pin him down, too. A remarkable fellow, Stanley. Halfway through his verse translation of the *Iliad*, a translation which

George had thought bid fair to be the best Englishing of Homer since Pope's and had said as much. In debate, Stanley knew how to use both sides of the sword, thwack with the flat of the blade, then the rapidissimo flash of the edge. Some cheap phrase-monger had called him the Rupert of debate and it had to be admitted he possessed a panache. Gladstone had said that at thirty Stanley was by far the cleverest young man of the day and at sixty he would still be by far the cleverest young man of the day. It was hard to prise him away from the betting room at Newmarket where he was all too often to be found standing at his ease, legs akimbo, among the touts and ruffians and chancers, laying a wager on anything – that Buckle would make nine stone for the Guineas, that Lord Glasgow would not sneeze in the next five minutes, that Flo O'Reilly could not (no, that wager was best effaced from the betting book). But all the same, if you could attract his attention for long enough, Stanley had considerable powers of application. If he could only be made to prepare, if the Incident – George supposed it must be called the Pacifico Incident – could only catch his imagination, then he would make a gigantic irreparable breach in Palmerston's defences, and George could pursue the attack in his own sober, stilted yet tenacious way until at last the British public could be made to understand what manner of man they had as their Foreign Secretary.

And Stanley did catch the Pacifico bug. There was

about it that combination of high principle and low farce which tickled his restless fancy. He spoke for two hours and more to an entranced House so crowded that some peeresses had to sit on the floors, their skirts plumped out like the plumage of glittering swans. Their perfume floated down the steps of the woolsack between the red front benches, filling the nostrils of government and opposition leaders impartially.

Never had trifles been so elevated into matters of international importance, Stanley began; never had unnecessary complications been accumulated with such a lavish expenditure of misdirected ingenuity. Greece was a newly created kingdom and an even newer constitutional monarchy. Instead of strengthening the authority and independence of the government of their new creation, the three great powers had been intriguing and caballing amongst themselves. Instead of behaving as a British Minister accredited to the court of Greece, Sir Edmund Lyons had been acting as the head of a party hostile to the existing government and using every possible means to displace it from office. His policy had been to exact reparations first and demand explanation afterwards, and all this irritating course of action had been sanctioned by Lord Palmerston in Downing Street.

After all, what were all these grievances which had provoked the despatch of this mighty fleet? There was the case of Stellio Sumachi, the burglarious blacksmith. The British passport he had obtained as an

Ionian subject was about the only thing he had come by honestly. Sumachi claimed to have been tortured in Patras when accused of robbery. Lord Palmerston immediately demanded the instant dismissal of the officers concerned in the outrage and adequate pecuniary compensation for Sumachi. Meanwhile, a court found that the torture story was a complete fiction from beginning to end. One would have thought that this would have been a staggerer to Lord Palmerston. No such thing. He went on demanding more inquiries.

Then there was the case of the *Fantome* which claimed that her crew had been manhandled and demanded compensation for the loss of a boathook. HMS *Spitfire* was sent to issue peremptory demands and bloodcurdling threats to the natives. Was there ever such a mountain made out of a molehill? Then there were the Ionian proprietors of a coffee shop at Patras who had been arrested (but then speedily released) for refusing to take down some flags which were causing a disturbance. Then there was the estimable historian, Mr Finley, a Scotsman with his countrymen's eye for a bargain, who had bought two-thirds of an acre from a Turkish gentleman and had then had the land taken by the government to be enclosed in King Otho's new garden. For years, Mr Finlay had been quietly pursuing his claim for compensation through the normal channels, when all at once the British fleet appeared off Athens to demand instant reparation. In fact, the claim had already been settled to Mr Finlay's satisfaction by the time Admiral Parker hove into view at the Piraeus.

And finally there was Don Pacifico. Now the peculiar circumstance in this case was that Don Pacifico did not seem to have a farthing. There was evidence laid before their lordships that he had been unable to redeem a piece of plate valued at thirty pounds which he had lodged with the Bank of Athens as a surety for a modest advance. More remarkable still, in the claims he was pursuing against the *Portuguese* government, he had claimed that their refusal to accede to his reasonable demands had left him poor and indigent.

Yet now he was putting in a claim for thirty-one thousand pounds and a claim which went into most precise and extensive detail.

'But, my lords, either M. Pacifico must be a man of the most extraordinary and accurate powers of memory that I ever heard of, or else, amidst this universal destruction, the plunderers must have been obliging enough to leave behind them a precise inventory of every item of furniture, and the value of each. My lords, no upholsterer's catalogue can be more complete than that which occupies some pages of the Blue Book on your lordships' table, enumerating, in the minutest detail, every article in M. Pacifico's house, from the sofas and chairs in the drawing-room, to the stew-pans, the jelly moulds, the skimming ladles in the kitchen. Every article, too, in its proper place; in such a box so many coats and other articles of Mr Pacifico's; in such a cupboard, so many gowns of Mrs Pacifico's, so many silk stockings of Miss Pacifico's, with all the minutiae of male and female apparel, into which I will not venture to follow the enumeration. Then the description of the furniture! Why, the house of this M. Pacifico, this petty usurer, who, as I have said, was trading on a borrowed capital of thirty pounds, is represented to have been furnished as luxuriously as it might have been if he had been another Aladdin with full command of the Genii of the ring and of the lamp. Now listen to the account of a single couch in his drawing room:

' "One large couch in solid mahogany, British work, with double bottom, one of which in Indian cane for summer, seventy pounds; one bottom for the winter for the above, a cushion in tapestry embroidered in real gold (Royal work), twenty-five pounds; two pillows and cushion also, for the back of the whole length of the couch, in silk and wool covering, embroidered in real gold, as the bottom of the above couch, seventy-five pounds."

'Total for one couch: one hundred and seventy pounds. Now, I doubt if many of your lordships have in your houses (I am sure I have not in mine) furniture of this gorgeous description. The bedroom is furnished on a scale of equal magnificence. In the first place appears a *lit conjugal* (I prefer the original to the

more homely translation of a "double-bed") of which
the following description is given:

' "A *lit conjugal*, in solid mahogany, with four
pillars richly carved, two and three-quarter feet long
by two and a quarter wide, with the back and the end
carved, the crown in carved mahogany and carved
frame, and a set of brass castors, worth one hundred
and fifty pounds." '

The jelly moulds and the *lit conjugal* were the
crowners. The House giggled and shook its sides.
Even old Lord Lansdowne, put up to defend the
indefensible for the government, smiled wide enough
to show what teeth he had left.

George did not need to lighten his own speech with
such detail – except to give a brief account of Admiral
Parker's malign odyssey around the Mediterranean:
stirring up both parties at Lisbon into a frenzy of
indignation, moving on to Naples to undermine the
King by first encouraging and then betraying the
Sicilian insurgents, then sailing on to the Ionian
Islands where the only service appears to have been to
satisfy the governor's requests for a supply of 'cats' to
flog the rebels, then taking the unbelievable and futile
step of passing through the Dardanelles to bring the
Emperor of Russia to agree with the Sultan, which he
had already done, and so we had had to apologise to
the Emperor, disavow Admiral Parker and pretend
that he had been driven through the straits by bad
weather. And what was the upshot?

'We may become used to anything, but our relations with the Great Powers of Europe are unprecedented, and cannot continue long without danger.' All these transactions cannot have taken place without more or less injuring the understanding which had formerly existed. Like all statesmen out of office, George could not resist looking back but four short years when this country was 'honoured, loved and respected by every state in Europe, with an intimate, a cordial good understanding with France' (the phrase went so sweetly into French too) and without the slightest diminution of our intimacy and friendship with all other powers. But now there were sore feelings on all sides. 'Unfortunately, it is a melancholy characteristic of human nature that we are apt to hate those whom we have much injured. I see symptoms of hate on the part of this country.' Luckily, people in other nations were able to separate the country from the government and were able to do justice to the private feeling of the people of England.

He sat down with a feeling of contentment such as he had experienced only once or twice in his life after a speech. Stanley's motion sailed through quite easily, with a majority of thirty-seven, and they sauntered off to Boodles like young bucks rather than weathered statesmen. It was only after dining, as they walked together up Whitehall, past Will Wilkins's National Gallery, up Haymarket, and on along Nash's great curving boulevard (for Derby House and Argyll

House were only a long stone's throw apart) – only then did dissatisfaction begin to tweak at his tired brain.

The happy glare of the red benches and Pugin's gilt pinnacles and rosy-cheeked peers congratulating one another on their brilliance – all that vanished in the cool midnight air, and George knew that he had not said all that he wanted to say, all that he felt he had been put on earth to say, all that forty years had taught him to say. And with each stride the dissatisfaction became a little more irritating, like a pebble lodged in his shoe, so that by the time their ways parted, just beyond the curve in Regent Street, he had become gruff, almost surly. Stanley looked at him and clapped him on the shoulder:

'Ye'll come on to Derby House for a nightcap, we cannot let such a night pass without a final libation.'

'I fear I should be poor company for your lordship.'

'My lord –' But Stanley looked again at the sturdy square figure like a Scotch minister in his funeral suit, and caught sight in the glare of the new gas lights of the mutinous melancholy on that old monkey face, and did not press the invitation. Besides, Aberdeen was indeed poor company after dark nowadays; he had even lost the taste for classical antiquities – 'ancient rubbish', he called them now – and Stanley wanted to be gay and recall the laughter that the jelly mould and the *lit conjugal* had brought. Never had he seen a jollier House, never – but he let Aberdeen go and went on home.

Two days later, Pam seemed to be done for. Pacifico's damages were reduced to six thousand four hundred pounds. Pam himself offered to resign; the Queen, most of the House of Lords and almost every sensible man in politics wanted him to go. But the Foreign Secretary's scalp was not a sufficient sacrifice. It was the government that had been defeated in the Lords and it was the government that had to fight back. They had to stick together or go together. So when Disraeli asked the Prime Minister whether they would resign, Lord John had to say that they would not, that they would seek a vote of confidence; and, as for the Foreign Secretary, he would answer for him that he would act not as the Minister of Austria, or 'the Minister of Russia, or of France, or of any other country, but as the Minister of England'. The patriotic card had been thumped down on the table. Blood was up and the game was on.

Never had George felt more sharply the difference between the two Houses. A week had passed, a week which had sharpened rather than appeased feelings; you could feel the abrasion in the air, and instead of two or three hundred lords there were six hundred of them, hotheads, radicals, loudmouths, braggarts, ingrates. Only on the backmost of the back benches squeezed under the galleries could you find dozy members like those who made up the soft cushioning of the Upper House. And even they were baying for foreign blood. Radical Roebuck had the House seething within twenty minutes. It was one of his best slashing brutal assaults. He lost no time in mocking the Queen's penchant for 'our dear Aberdeen', compared the maltreatment of Don Pacifico to the maltreatment of Shylock, reproved the Upper House for their levity in regard to the *lit conjugal*, roasted the French, bastinadoed the Russians, and demanded clear and unambiguous approval for this motion so that the government might continue to 'have the power to maintain the dignity of this country in the face of the world'.

By comparison, Pam started off judicious and grave. But by Jove, he was long. George saw Sir Robert nod off for a full hour by Pugin's clock and Lord John fast asleep for as long. Four hours and more they had of it. If he was to be accused of being incapable of temperate and courteous action, if he was to be charged with 'running amuck through Europe', then he was going to supply his accusers with an answer they would not forget. Their lordships might treat these incidents lightly, they might be kept on a roar of laughter for an hour together at the poverty of one sufferer or at the miserable habitation of another, at the nationality of one injured man or the religion of another, as if because a man was poor he might be bastinadoed and tortured with impunity, or because a man is of the Jewish persuasion, he is fair game for any outrage. Those innocent Ionian coffee sellers had been arrested and manacled and thumbscrewed and in that state paraded through the town. It was said that they had been released the next day, and that because the thumbscrews had not maimed them for life no compensation ought to be paid. His lordship was of a different opinion. Thumbscrews were not as easy to wear as gloves which can be put on and pulled off at pleasure.

As it happened, Mr Finlay's claim had *not* been settled by the time Admiral Parker hove in view. In fact, he had not received a penny. And Pam knew nothing of the truth or falsehood of the stories about Mr Pacifico. He didn't care what Mr Pacifico's character was. Because a man may have acted amiss on some other occasions, he was not to be wronged with impunity now. And how was he to obtain redress? The courts of Greece were not like our courts. Mr Pacifico himself had truly said that 'if the man I prosecute is rich, he is sure to be acquitted; if he is poor, he has nothing out of which to afford me compensation'.

It was said that Greece was a small country, a weak country, and that it was an ungenerous proceeding to employ so large a force against so small a power. But did the smallness of a country justify the magnitude of its evil acts? If we had sent merely a frigate or a sloop, we should have placed them in a more undignified position by asking them to yield to so small a demonstration (leaning over the rail of the peers' gallery, George's monkey face twitched at the thought that Cupid had been considering the feelings of the

Greek ministry in despatching Parker's Armada to the Piraeus). Admiral Parker had been unjustly traduced. A fleet at the mouth of the Dardanelles could be a threat to nobody.

It had always been the fate of advocates of temperate reform to be run at as the fomenters of revolution. In France, in Switzerland, he gave advice calculated to prevent revolutions by reconciling opposite parties and conflicting views. His was a policy of improvement and peace. We had shown the example of a nation in which every class of society accepts with cheerfulness the lot which Providence has assigned to it (another grim smile from the monkey face peering over the railing). The question was whether as the Roman in days of old held himself free from indignity when he could say *civis romanus sum*, so also a British subject, in whatever land he may be, shall feel confident that the watchful eye and the strong arm of England will protect him against injustice and wrong.

There had never been such a triumph. The government benches erupted, great molten streams of patriotic feeling flowed over them, crushing all doubts and qualifications under tons of glowing clinker. Pacifico was avenged, he was clasped to our bosom, our infinitely expansive, boundlessly generous bosom (he came to settle in the City of London and made his final flit, to the Spanish cemetery in Mile End, four years later). And the warm heart beating indomitably behind the bosom was Cupid, with his dyed whiskers and his quenchless amorosity – never was beef roast like him.

There were two more nights to come; there was Sidney Herbert to speak, and Gladstone and Grey and Cobden and Lord John, and Disraeli to wind up. But it was all over, the majority was in the bag, a highly respectable majority of forty-six, the government was safe and Palmerston was safer still, safe in the affections of the public, that new alarming personage which had to be reckoned with, which insisted on going into dinner before dukes and archbishops and on monopolising the conversation so that sanity and moderation could not get a word in. Public opinion did not want to be told that the Romans who were so proud of their citizenship were in fact an oppressor race tyrannising most of the known world. Public opinion did not want to be told that, outside England, the Pacifico affair was regarded (not least by the French) as a triumph for the French, who had been trying to negotiate a peaceful settlement from the beginning. Public opinion did not want to be told anything, it knew what it liked and what it liked was Palmerston. MPs were swamped by letters from their constituents. Pam sat for portraits and was interminably entertained to nine-course dinners at which all the verses of God Save the Queen were sung and eighty-one different dishes were served. And Pam soared on: Britain would always support the cause of freedom throughout the world, no nation was any more eager to go to war with Britain than Britain was to go to war with it. Ah, the flagons of champagne that were consumed in freedom's name, the bumpers of port that coupled the toast with the name of England's Pam.

And Lord Aberdeen? The sadness was so settled on his monkey face that you might have thought nothing could deepen the melancholy that clung to him. But something did, and it was not even the triumph of Lord Palmerston.

Halfway through the last night of the Pacifico debate, the one great man in the Commons who had not yet spoken rose to his feet: that big figure in the long blue frock coat and white waistcoat with his long shambling legs, and his long limp arms, and his cold bright blue eyes.

'Sir Robert Peel.'

He started slow and quiet with his hands clasped behind him under his coat-tails as he always did. Tonight, he was mulling, reflective. He was not hunting for votes, he did not seek to overthrow the ministry he had supported for four years and with which he had so much in common. Of course Mr Pacifico had as good a right to redress as any British nobleman but his claims could have been settled without bullying Greece or offending France or Russia. What, after all, was diplomacy for?

'It is a costly engine for maintaining peace. It is a remarkable instrument used by civilised nations for the purpose of preventing war. Unless it is used to appease the angry passions of individual men, to check the feelings that rise out of national resentments . . . it is an instrument not only costly but mischievous. If then your application of diplomacy be to fester every wound, to provoke instead of soothing resentments, to place a minister in every court of Europe for the purpose, not of preventing quarrels, or of adjusting quarrels, but for the purpose of continuing an angry correspondence, and for the purpose of promoting what is supposed to be an English intestest . . . then I say, that not only is the expenditure upon this costly instrument thrown away, but this great engine, used by civilised society for the purpose of maintaining peace, is perverted into a cause of hostility and war.'

Was it really right to use the moral influence of the British government to support any body of men anywhere who were struggling to achieve self-government against their legitimate rulers? What was the basis of this self-government – monarchical or republican? Did it apply to India, to China? Mr Fox, Mr Pitt, Mr Canning and Lord Castlereagh had all held that the true policy of this country was non-intervention in the affairs of others – unless some clear and undeniable British interest was at stake. Had they all been wrong? Surely constitutional liberty would be best worked out by those who aspire to freedom by their own efforts.

When Sir Robert sat down, and tipped his tall hat over his broad brow and began fiddling with the gold seals on his watch-chain again, up in the peers' gallery George felt a great sense of relief flood in upon him. The debate was lost, the government had survived, but Peel, his old colleague, his old master, so long half estranged, had said the things he knew he had failed to say himself. The true policy of England had been set out by her greatest statesman.

After the debate, George tried to catch a word with him, but Peel was already gone halfway up Whitehall with his long legs moving in their peculiar stately shamble, Peel's two left legs as O'Connell called them, the feet almost sliding over the pavement. By the time the rest of them had passed Downing Street, he was round the corner and out of sight.

The next morning, Peel went to a long committee meeting on the arrangements for the Great Exhibition. At five o'clock, he went out for his usual ride in the Park. The horse was an eight-year-old which had been bought for him at Tattersalls a couple of months earlier. Peel's own coachman thought it an ugly animal, and told him not to ride it, but Sir Robert did not always take advice even from his coachman, and he liked a spirited hack. First he called at Buckingham Palace and wrote his name in the visitors' book, then he rode at a walk up Constitution Hill. Just as he came in sight of St. George's Hospital, half-hidden by the trees, the horse began to buck and plunge. He was greeting Lady Dover and her two daughters and was vexed that he had his hands too full to doff his hat. Sir Robert fell face downwards at full length still holding the reins. The horse stumbled on top of him, striking him on the back with its knees. He died two nights later of pneumonia caused by a fractured rib. As he lay dying, crowds of working people packed Whitehall Gardens and the streets surrounding. The popular mourning was greater than for any statesman since Pitt. George thought the feeling for Peel was even more genuine and widespread.

Something had gone out of England, gone for ever, perhaps. What it was he could not quite say, but whatever it was Gladstone did not have it and Disraeli certainly did not have it, and none of the younger men had an inkling of it. What was it? A kind of modesty perhaps, he could not be sure. A sense that England had its place and that politics had their place – honoured places but places that were bounded in time and space and power and ought to be so bounded. That was all over now. There were no limits left to England's glory. And Peel was gone and Aberdeen was left behind.

The day after Sir Robert's fall, George was at Blackheath. He stood on the hearthrug and talked of indifferent matters. 'Why does grandpapa stand so very still today?' the children asked. That night, he was attacked by violent, almost unbearable spasms in his stomach and the old flashes of pain at his temple.

— VII —

He had taken to eating his porridge standing upright in the Scotch manner. While he ate with his long Jacobite silver spoon from the horn porringer, he would shift from one foot to the other (was it his coat-tails or his shoes that made that stiff rustling, a noise so marked that Mary Haddo could hear whether her father-in-law was breakfasting while she was still out in the passage?). And as he ate, he liked to read a newspaper or a book which would be propped on a high wooden music stand set in the light of the window, for his eyes were dimming and even with spectacles newspaper print still read small. Now and then, he would look out of the window and across the hummocky slopes of Greenwich and Blackheath, with the black ant columns of city clerks marching off to work through the low old oaks with the spidery dew still on them. After Bentley was no longer his to live in, the Queen had given her dear Lord Aberdeen the use of the Ranger's House, and he had become as fond of it as his sadly depleted heart was capable of, and Mary too he loved, despite her prissy Evangelical reproaches – in fact, he rather relished those, they made him feel almost frisky.

'What's this? *Britons, guard your own.* It sounds like advice from Thomas Cook. *Prenez garde à vos bagages. Now practise, yeomen, like those bowmen* – was there ever a patriotic poem that could resist rhyming yeomen with bowmen? – *till your balls fly as their true shafts have flown, yeomen, guard your own.* I never read such stuff, Mary, why have you inflicted this doggerel on me? I'm surprised the *Examiner* printed it.'

'I have it on very good authority that it is by Mr Tennyson, my lord.'

'I can't believe it. Well, if it is, I'm not surprised he didn't care to put his name to it.'

'He feels very strongly about Louis Napoleon, Lady Alice says.'

'Does he now? And does Lady Alice feel strongly too?'

'Oh my lord, you must not make game of me.'

She did not like his irony. Not many people did. Even to those he loved, it came out like sarcasm. And when he was on his hindlegs in public, it made too acid an impression, particularly for that emollient assembly where fate had plumped him.

'Mary, why is the *Examiner* on my stand again this week?'

'There is another poem I think you should read, my lord. It is an answer to Lord Stanley – I mean Lord Derby's remarks last week.'

'All he said was, if we wanted to get on with Louis Napoleon, it would do no harm to keep a civil tongue in our heads. *My lords, we heard you speak . . . if you be fearful, then must we be bold. Our Britain cannot salve a tyrant o'er . . . We broke them on the land, we drove them on the seas . . . Is this the manly strain of Runnymede?* Heaven preserve us, this is worse than the last one. Signed *Merlin*. Am I to suppose . . . ?'

'Lady Alice says Mrs Tennyson persuaded him not to sign it with his own name, so as not to upset the Queen.'

'I imagine the next effusion will be signed Guinevere.'

'Mrs Tennyson says he has also written several poems urging the formation of volunteer rifle clubs, although he does not wish these to be published for the moment, but he has sent ten pounds to Mr Patmore, who has founded such a club, I understand.'

'When poets join the press gang, I fear it must be all up with us. Well, I remember old Sheridan drilling his volunteers in St. James' Park, but Tennyson forming squares! I hope they don't fix bayonets or he'll skewer that great hat of his.'

'You told me once you wore a red coat at Leipzig.'

'So I did and a fine fellow I felt too, I must admit, but there was a war on then. Have these distinguished gentlemen noticed that we are not actually at war with France, at least we weren't yesterday?'

'Did you not also tell me once, my lord, that strong preparation is the foundation of a sound foreign policy?'

'There is a difference between preparation and provocation. In any case, *si vis pacem, para bellum* is a maxim that has done more harm than any other I can think of, except possibly take no thought for the morrow.'

'My lord, I do not care for it when you plunder the Scriptures for your chaffing.'

But he turned towards her and took off his reading glasses and mustered one of his old monkey grins, appealed – successfully – to her affection for him. It was a kind of moral admiration, one which she could not honestly feel for her invalid husband George the younger, who had lately become obsessed with the notion that society's ills were largely due to the employment of nude models in art classes (and later was to spend much time in Egypt trying to convert the Copts to the Evangelical faith).

George could not pretend, though, that he was not depressed by this muddy surge of patriotic verse. He could smell the war fever steaming up from it as well as any man. The sickly choking urgency was every-where. He did not need actually to witness Mr

Patmore's poets drilling on some blasted heath to see what was coming – and coming to him.

A becoming show of reluctance had to be made, of course. No man had more experience of that than he. After all, who else had been refusing embassies and ministries for forty years, who else had more often declared that he would prefer to plant trees in Aberdeenshire than pump out *aide-mémoires* in Whitehall? He was the Cincinnatus emeritus.

'My lord, profoundly flattered though I undoubtedly am by your suggestion, I ought to make it entirely clear that in my present state of health, and with my private preoccupation, the last thing in my thoughts is that I should . . .' There were many such letters to be written that summer and autumn, but there was nobody else and he knew it, and the upshot was that he found himself, not entirely to his surprise or reluctance, dragged into the highest office of all before Christmas, and there began to preside over what showed bright early promise. This Peelite-conservative administration was worthy to bear the honoured name (albeit hyphenated) of Sir Robert: Gladstone as Chancellor, Lord John at the Foreign Office, Palmerston at the Home Office – Mr Bagehot was not alone in thinking George's Cabinet the ablest they had had since the Reform Act. True, there was something a little odd about its composition – heavily Peelite, especially in the great offices of state, when there were two hundred and seventy Whigs and

Radicals and less than three dozen Peelites in the House of Commons. Still, odder *mélanges* than that had worked.

And how they worked. They started off at a gallop. Gladstone's first budget, three hours of it, like the flow of some great crystal stream, reduced income tax, slashed the stamp duty on newspapers, taxed the well-to-do across the water, abolished the excise duty on soap, and a dozen other things. Wood's India Bill introduced competitive exams for the Indian Civil Service and, horror of horrors, a legislative council to advise the Governor-General. True, there would only be Europeans on it to start with, but it could only be a matter of time before natives elbowed their way in there, just as it would only be a matter of time before competitive exams were introduced for the British Civil Service also – and not very much time either, for within six months Sir Charles Trevelyan and Sir Stafford Northcote were put to enquire into the good old patronage system. Pushing seventy, George found himself in the not entirely disagreeable role of imposing meritocracy on Old Corruption.

As for Cupid – not previously regarded as a friend to reform – never was such a wondrous reformation seen in Whitehall. The road to Damascus witnessed only the mildest of deviations by comparison. The new Home Secretary prohibited all labour by young persons between six pm and six am; he stopped employers from diddling their workers by paying them in goods rather than cash; he persuaded the government to support compulsory vaccination; he moved the first Smoke Abatement Bill, which began to tug at the dirty black coverlet of coalsmoke which had hung over London for two centuries; he ended the insanitary practice of burying the dead in churches rather than churchyards; he ended transportation to Australia; he had half a mind to stop the working classes drinking, too.

George encouraged and nudged and approved. These were not his fields, but he was happy to lean on the gate and watch them grow. His expertise lay further afield, in pastures he had tramped and tilled for forty years: the parched thickets of Anglo–French relations, always liable to burst into flames at the drop of a lighted match; the pink and white and ochre mosques and spires of Bosnia where he had wandered when young; the heathery hills of Ireland; the holy places of Palestine; and, above all, the headlands of the Hellespont with their brisk winds whipping up from the plains of Troy. Was there anyone else who knew them better, these earthquake zones of the civilised world in which a slumbrous peace could be shattered in a day because they lay above the fault lines in human history: the crack between Protestants and Catholics, between Catholics and Orthodox, between Orthodox and Moslems? Unceasing vigilance, inexhaustible tact, slowness to wrath, all those qualities were needed, but above all one had to understand, to have experienced the history and to know the present reality. No other active statesman in Europe could match him in that. Guizot was out, Metternich was old; and besides, even in their prime they were a little too cynical to understand the incompleteness of *realpolitik*. A statesman needed a moral heart as well as an undeceived mind.

So when the Eastern Question arose once again, as inevitably as the sun, he met it with the old answers and he met it with confidence. In three administrations, over a period of forty years, he had helped bring his country to peace and help her at peace. That induces a certain self-confidence in a man, and George was not by nature underendowed with self-confidence.

He had seen it all before. Louis Napoleon claimed rights over the Holy Places for the Catholics, he sent a warship through the Dardanelles, the Tsar asked the Sultan to reaffirm his Treaty rights, the Tsar threatened to occupy the Danubian principalities, the French fleet moved to the Dardanelles, a British fleet kept pace with it. Notes flew to and fro – the Menshikov Ultimatum, the Vienna Note, the Olmutz proposals.

'This is alarming news, papa,' Mary would say as she settled the newspaper on the black wooden stand.

'Oh, I think it is only the Queen's Pawn Gambit,' he would reply, 'or the French Defence. I think we should be able to stalemate it without too much difficulty.'

One day in the summer, he had news that the Russians had signed the Vienna Note.

'It is all settled, my dear.'

'Settled, you mean, for good.' She looked at the happiness spread over the monkey face and needed no answer.

But the Turks rejected the Vienna Note and then it emerged that the Russians took a peculiar and sinister view of it, and sadness settled on him with the autumn. By September, he was writing to Mary.

'I am sorry to say that the political prospect is very gloomy, and that it is becoming worse and worse. There is a general desire of war, or, as it is called, supporting the honour of the country, which it will be difficult to resist' – it was not the Russians or the Turks who were the trouble, it was the city clerks striding off to Mincing Lane with war in their hearts, warrior ants now – 'I shall personally continue my pacific policy as long as I am able, but when I am overborne, as I see that I shall be, I will readily leave the execution of a different policy to others.'

Why didn't he then? Why didn't he up sticks and head north, when, as Palmerston pointed out, the Olmutz proposals for peace turned out to be mere 'après dîner moutarde' and war was an undodgable reality and the sooner the British fleet was in the Black Sea the better? Why didn't he resign even when the Russians sank the Turkish squadron at Sinope in November? Why did he cling on and on, to office, to hopes of peace, to hopes of brief and token hostilities even after Britain had declared war (and that was not until the following March)?

Vanity, I expect, and the tears of the Queen who implored him to stay, and fear that Palmerston would widen the objects of war, up to and including a full-scale invasion of Russia. How much cleaner and nobler it would have looked if he had gone, how much more we would remember him (our memories are fuzzy and need sharp outlines).

But he didn't go. He stayed. He endured, and among the things he endured was one of the first great press onslaughts in history. He was the St. Stephen of the mass media, the first martyr. Perhaps he had it coming to him. After all there were parts of the modern world he only dimly apprehended: the dark mephitic vicious corners of it, those he had only a glimmering of; he could not see how the contagion could spread to the well-scrubbed warrior ants walking past his windows, he could not see who Dizzy was writing for in his weekly, *The Press*:

'Lord Aberdeen's mind, his education, his prejudices are all of the Kremlin school. Now that he is placed in a prominent position, and forced to lead English gentlemen, instead of glozing and intriguing with foreign diplomatists, not a night passes that his language or his demeanour does not shock and jar upon the frank and genial spirit of our British Parliament. His manner, arrogant and yet timid – his words, insolent and yet obscure – offend even his political supporters. His hesitating speech, his contracted sympathies, his sneer, icy as Siberia, his sarcasms, drear and barren as the Steppes, are all characteristic of the bureau and the chancery, and not of popular and aristocratic assemblies animated by the spirit of honour and the pride of gentlemen. If war breaks out – and the present prospect is that war will break out – this dread calamity must be placed to the account of this man, and of this man alone.'

And that had been in June when George was still riding high and it still seemed he might once again find an answer to the Eastern Question.

He was hurt, he did not think it worth denying he was hurt, certainly not to Mary (she was an ever more comforting confidante, not least because there was a certain evangelical denseness to her, so that he could play his thoughts and anxieties off her as though she were the wall of a fives court). But he was puzzled too. Of course, Disraeli did not care for him – he was, after all, a remnant of the Peelites Dizzy had persecuted for so long and, as George himself had pointed out in the Pacifico debate, we are apt to hate those whom we have injured. Yet he had not personally injured Disraeli. Not a week since, he had voted for the Jewish Disabilities Bill, indeed had introduced it himself to the House of Lords. And he had been fond of old Isaac, that scholarly magpie. There came to him a curiously distinct recollection of a frosty morning on the steps of the Society of Antiquaries when Isaac had pushed forward a moony gangling youth with huge eyes brimming with suspicion and a large sloppy humorous mouth and said, in an unlikely biblical way, 'This is my son Benjamin.' No, why should Disraeli be so vicious, why should he degrade legitimate disagreement into a near-criminal attack on George's honour?

Mr Disraeli knew in his bones what later generations of propaganda masters had to teach themselves, that repetition is the thing that counts. The following week's issue of *The Press* returned to the attack:

'The curse of "antiquated imbecility" has fallen in all its fullness, on Lord Aberdeen. His temper, naturally morose, has become licentiously peevish. Crossed in his Cabinet, he insults the House of Lords, and plagues the most eminent of his colleagues with the crabbed malice of a maundering witch.'

Well, George knew he had himself partly to blame. He could not bluster to save his life. As public indignation swelled, his speeches in the House of Lords became ever more temperate and reasonable – and, alas, stumbling. He was old now and a little deaf and his old nerves came back. Palmerston's white-stockinged legs sprawled across the steps of the throne, the sudden dizziness and banging at the temples, the sandy Scotch peer who had pointed the little door to the privy – there was no such easy way out now. But when he rose from the front bench to proclaim the majestic wrath of England, he simply couldn't do it, he could not help setting out the policy of Russia in the most understanding fashion. Even when actually declaring war, he could not help adding, 'I make peace my first object and my first vow.' Had not Fairfax, the nonpareil of the Civil War, continued to murmur, 'Peace, peace!' while arming himself for battle? But who wanted to hear that sort of language? Certainly not the Queen. She understood what Lord Aberdeen meant, of course she did, but 'the public is impatient and annoyed to hear at this moment the first Minister of the Crown enter into an *impartial* examination of the Emperor of Russia's character and conduct.'

And so on and on it went, traitor, tool of the Kremlin, coward – and others joined the chorus, Sir Robert's old ally the *Morning Chronicle*, the radical *Daily News*, the Conservative *Morning Herald*, and eventually *The Times*. He had thought Mr Delane was a sensible young man, *The Times* had been regarded as the most steadfast supporter of the coalition and of Lord Aberdeen personally. For years they had met privately and chatted, when Delane was still in his early twenties and the youngest man on *The Times*' staff as well as being the Editor. Though Delane had a tendresse for Pam and shared his preference for charging at life, he had a genuine fondness and respect for George. When Lord Aberdeen was Foreign Secretary, he would share secrets with Mr Delane, and the readers of *The Times* would share them too. Above all, Delane hated war, saw all the futility and horror of it; he liked military manoeuvres, would spend his days of leisure riding about with the troops on manoeuvre on Salisbury Plain or on the wastes of Aldershot, but he was under no illusion about the realities of combat.

'There's a young Irishman I would like you to meet, my lord.'

'What, younger than you, Delane?'

'We *Times* men age fast, my lord. I feel middle-aged already, but Mr Russell will never grow old. He is an Irish journalist, the most youthful breed of men known to science. I am despatching him to the Crimea.'

'Are you, indeed? I hope he will report truthfully upon the campaign.'

William Howard Russell landed at Gallipoli at the beginning of April 1854, when the irises and anemones were just coming out. It was the most fateful landing on that tawny windswept peninsula when the stout pop-eyed Irish reporter stepped ashore, the most fateful since ancient times (although Gallipoli had more in store).

War with Russia had been officially declared a month earlier. But earlier still, in January, Princess Lieven, safely back in Paris now, had written her last letter to him: 'to think that we should have come to this, with *you* governing England. *Adieu, mon cher* Lord Aberdeen, *mon cher ennemi*.' After it was all over, everyone, even Disraeli, would agree that it was a just war, but an unnecessary one. But it now seemed to George that he was almost the last person in Britain who was unpersuaded of its necessity – and the only person who thought he could have stopped it. Others might have supported him, true. 'I believe that there were in the course of the negotiations two occasions when, if I had been supported, peace might have been honourably and advantageously secured. But I repeat that the want of support, though it may palliate, cannot justify to my own conscience the course which I pursued.'

Oh that conscience, he was always going on about it, especially to Lord John Russell: 'My conscience upbraids me the more because it is possible by a little more energy and vigour, not on the Danube, but in Downing Street, it might have been prevented.' Lord John, as it happened, was not a man for such finicky considerations, but even Gladstone, who liked to give his conscience a regular airing, thought George was wrong to take the blame. The war had come about through the natural evolution of the concert of Europe: one nation had broken the rules and had to be punished. And, in any case, Lord Aberdeen never had the votes. Two hundred and seventy war-crazed Whigs and Radicals, barely thirty pacific Peelites – that was the brutal parliamentary arithmetic, and even the most scrupulous of consciences must allow itself to be silenced by the arithmetic. But George's conscience would not stay quiet. A week before the other Russell landed at Gallipoli, he wrote to John Bright: 'I feel as if every drop of blood that is to be shed will rest upon my head.'

To start with, he had to confess it, he rather enjoyed Mr Russell's despatches. They were vivid, a little florid now and then perhaps, over-jocular possibly. But they conveyed, as a good journalist should, something of the exhilaration of a great expedition setting out and something of the grandeur of the voyage through the Mediterranean – the storms sweeping over the fickle sea, a violent indigo stippled with patches of white foam, the rugged mountains of the Greek coast with their peaks soaring straight out of the sea (Mount Athos a pyramid of purple cloud bathed in golden light). The very names of Her Majesty's ships bathed the enterprise in a classical glow – the *Golden Fleece*, the *Leander*. They anchored in the bays of the Peloponnese, and the bands played dance music, and at the end the mountains of the Morea echoed to the strains of God Save the Queen – for the first time since the birth of Venus, Mr Russell said in a sweeping way, as if before then the National Anthem was often to be heard in those parts.

George had found Mr Russell in person a little too – what? bumptious, full of himself? But he could not deny that he wrote with brio. All the time he was trying to stop this wretched war, Mr Russell's hearty bouncing prose was making him feel young again, making him wish he was standing in the prow of *HMS Leander* with the spray on his cheek and watching dawn come up over the Dardanelles, that cold silvery dawn that made you feel a little sick, part with hunger, part with beauty.

There were a few grumbles on the voyage but nothing out of the usual run of soldiers' curses and the unavoidable hitches and shortcomings that attend all military excursions. It was Mr Russell's despatch of 13 April that first sounded a new sharper note.

'The men suffer exceedingly from cold. Some of them, officers as well as privates, have no beds to lie on. None of the soldiers have more than their single regulation blanket. They therefore reverse the order of things, and dress to go to bed, putting on all their spare clothes and warm clothing before they try to sleep. The worst thing I have to report is the continued want of comforts for the sick. Many of the men labouring under diseases contracted at Malta are obliged to stay in camp in the cold, with only one blanket under them, as there is no provision for them at the temporary hospital.'

Well, surely that want could be attended to. Newcastle must attend to it; assured him, assured the House of Lords a fortnight later, that he had attended to it. But here was that cocksure Russell not accepting His Grace's word.

'No, I repeat it, there were no blankets for the sick, no beds, no mattresses, no medical comforts of any kind, and the invalid soldiers had to lie for several days on the bare boards in a wooden house, with nothing but a single blanket as bed and covering. The Duke says he cannot but feel confident there was a proper supply of hospital tents on board the *Golden Fleece*; and further says, he directed two sailing transports to proceed to Gallipoli from Malta, should there be insufficient hospital accommodation on shore. I am afraid his confidence has been misplaced in the first place.'

Mr Russell was probably right. Newcastle was not up to the job. They all knew it, shifted in their seats as the poor fellow attempted to give Cabinet yet another military *tour d'horizon*. He was old, too old, they were all too old. Raglan was sixty-five, Admiral Dundas was seventy, Sir John Burgoyne was seventy-two, half the general staff had fought against Napoleon. Several of them kept on forgetting and referring to the enemy as 'the Frenchies'. But it was too late to promote their juniors, too late to repair the neglect of thirty years, too late to educate the officers in the elementaries of war, like sanitation.

'In the stagnant water which ripples almost imperceptibly on the shore there float all forms of nastiness and corruption, which the prowling dogs, standing leg-deep as they wade about in search of offal, cannot destroy. The smell from this shore is noisome, but a few yards out from the fringe of buoyant cats, dogs, birds, straw, sticks – in fact, of all sorts of abominable flotsam and jetsam, which bob about on the pebbles unceasingly – the water becomes exquisitely clear and pure. The slaughter-houses erected by the seaside do not contribute, as may readily be imagined, to the cleanliness of this filthy beach or the wholesomeness of the atmosphere.'

George knew what the consequences would be, had seen them for himself forty years earlier on the fetid fields of Bohemia. 'The cholera has crept from the camps into the town, and, as is usual on its outbreak, has exhibited great malignancy. On Monday, July 24th, it broke out in the camp of the Light Division. Upwards of twenty men died in twenty-four hours. A sergeant of the 88th was taken ill at seven o'clock, and was dead at twelve o'clock.'

What use were natural beauties now?

'Whoever gazed on these rich meadows, stretching for long miles away, and bordered by heights on which the dense forests struggled all but in vain to pierce the masses of wild vine, clematis, dwarf acacia, and many-coloured brushwoods – on the verdant hill-sides, and on the dancing waters of lake and stream below, lighted up by the golden rays of a Bulgarian summer's sun – might well think that no English glade or hill-top could well be healthier or better suited for the residence of man. But these meadows nurture the fever, the ague, dysentery, and pestilence in their bosom – the lake and the stream exhale death, and at night fat unctuous vapours rise up fold after fold from the valleys, and creep up in the dark and steal into the tent of the sleeper and wrap him in their deadly embrace. So completely exhausted, on last Thursday, was the Brigade of Guards, these three thousand of the flower of England, that they had to make two marches in order to get over the distance from Aladyn to Varna, which is not more than (not so much, many people say, as) ten miles. But that is not all. Their packs were carried for them. Just think of this, good people of England, who are sitting anxiously in your homes, day after day, expecting every morning to gladden your eyes with the sight of the announcement, in large type, of "Fall of Sebastopol", your Guards, your *corps d'élite*, the pride of your hearts, the delight of your eyes, these Anakim, whose stature, strength, and massive bulk you exhibit to kingly visitors as no inapt symbols of your nation, have been so reduced by sickness, disease, and a depressing climate, that it was judged inexpedient to allow them to carry their own packs, or to permit them to march more than five miles a day, even though these packs were carried for them! Think of this, and then judge whether these men are fit in their present state to go to Sebastopol, or to attempt any great operation of war.'

For God's sake, he needn't lay it on so thick. All wars had their horrors; disease always carried off just as many men as powder and shot. A correspondent on the field of battle was not called upon to shatter the morale of his fellow countrymen. That was surely not Mr Delane's purpose in sending him out there. What was Lord Raglan thinking of, allowing the fellow to wander all over the place? On and on he went.

'Walking by the beach, one sees some straw sticking up through the sand, and scraping it away with his stick, he is horrified at bringing to light the face of a corpse, which has been deposited there, with a wisp of straw around it, a prey to dogs and vultures. Dead bodies rise up from the bottom in the harbour, and bob grimly around in the water, or float in from sea, and drift past the sickened gazers on board the ships – all buoyant, bolt upright, and hideous, in the sun. On Friday, the body of a French soldier, who had been murdered (for his neckerchief was twisted round the neck so as to produce strangulation, and the forehead was laid open by a ghastly wound which cleft the skull to the brain), came alongside the *Caradoc* in harbour, and was with difficulty sunk again.'

That too he himself had seen a lifetime ago: the body of a young dragoon, strangely fair for a Frenchman, lying face up in a stagnant pond, a filthy liver-green bog, with his long fair hair rippling in the foulness at the splash of passing hooves but the face not moving. All that he had seen. At least perhaps this acquaintance with the realities of war would open the eyes of those who had not seen and who called so cheerfully for war, war and war again. Perhaps now that they had seats in the front row for Mr Russell's magic lantern show, perhaps now at last they would see that the game was not worth the candle. He made you see all right, this Russell, made you see the Light Cavalry teeming past in the glitter of the morning sun, the chink and jingle breaking the silence of the plain, then the smoke and the roar of the Russian batteries. You could still see the sabres flashing even through the thickening smoke, the silence again, then the dreadful chaos: screaming, running men, riderless horses, corpses trampled, the Russian gunners still firing, firing, firing on friend and foe alike. 'At thirty-five minutes past eleven,' ah that terrible precision, 'not a British soldier, except the dead and dying, was left in front of these bloody Muscovite guns.'

On and on it went, Russell's own remorseless cannonade, once a week, sometimes twice a week. And always with the same message: chaos, incompetence, neglect, blunder. Gloom settled over the dreadful peninsula, gloom and squalor and famine.

Only one lamp shone in the darkness. It was Palmerston who had introduced her: 'May I present the daughter of an old friend,' and a sharp-featured young woman, not attractive but forceful-looking, had shaken his hand. 'Mr Nightingale was my neighbour in Hampshire, seconded my nomination when I stood there. Miss Nightingale wants to go out.'

'Go out?'

'To Scutari, to nurse the soldiery.'

'I fear . . .'

'No place for a woman, you mean. You don't know Miss Nightingale.'

And looking into those fierce eyes – perhaps she was not so ill-featured after all – George could see immediately that he did not know Miss Nightingale, but he had a feeling that she knew Lord Palmerston, knew him through and through, from his whiskers to his spats, and would make what use of him she needed. Well, he liked to see Palmerston used, he had used so many men and women – especially women – that the whirligig of time was somewhat overdue.

But now Miss Nightingale had the Crimean fever herself and even that lamp was temporarily dimmed. Why this terrible listless silence? No drum, no bugle call ever roused the camp. But then so many of its inhabitants were past rousing.

'I have slept lately in a sunken hut in which a corpse lies buried, with only a few inches of earth between its head and my own. Within a yard and a half of the door of my present abode are the shallow graves of three soldiers, a little earth heaped up loosely over them, mixed with scanty lime, which does not even destroy the rank vegetation that springs out of them. Nearer still is a large mound, supposed to contain the remains of a camel – rather a large supply of noxious gases; and further away, at the distance of about a hundred and eighty yards, are the graves of the division, where hundreds of bodies lie lightly covered as close as they can pack.'

And he too was buried by the catastrophe, dumped as irremediably underground and as dead to posterity as if he had never lived. For Mr Russell's despatches did not open their eyes. Those bleary bloodshot orbs remained furiously narrowed. What Mr Russell's despatches did was to ignite their rage to a heat that no mortal statesman could have withstood.

He was hurrying home, the rain thrumming a dirge on his old umbrella, his heart numb, his dejection irreparable. Out of a filthy alley, a dark shape came at him.

'Evenin' sir, ballad, only a penny, latest,' it growled, in a strange deep, lisping voice.

'What is it?'

But the shape just thrust it into his hand and George found himself fumbling for his penny. As he shook the rain off his coat in the hall, he flattened the crumpled broadsheet on the little *pietra dura* table he had bought with Harriet on one of their happier days in Nice. A TUNE FOR LORD ABERDEEN was the title in blocky capital letters blurred by the rain.

> Yes our brave troops are dying,
> Coop'd up in heated camps
> Before they well can strike a blow
> At Russia's ragged scamps:
> And as with furrowed brows they ask
> 'What do our generals mean?'
> They curse, within their heart of hearts
> 'That coward, ABERDEEN!'

There were four more verses in the same vein. He sat down in the coachman's chair beside the table.

Later that week, men appeared outside his gates as night was falling. They came in purposeful groups, with a lantern, and at a signal from their leader broke into A Tune for Lord Aberdeen. They sang in hoarse, derisive voices and rattled the railings with their sticks. One or two of them ventured a step or two into the courtyard but ran off as soon as the porter came out of his lodge.

Not long after that, in the depths of winter, the irrepressible Roebuck had put his motion of censure on the government's conduct of the war, and the Commons passed it by a mile, and George caught the two o'clock train to Windsor in the snow and resigned his seals of office and the Queen took them from him with her pudgy little-girl's hands and tears in her eyes again.

A few weeks later, she insisted on conferring on him the vacant ribbon of the Garter. When he arrived at Windsor for the second time, he found a letter waiting for him.

'Though the Queen hopes to see Lord Aberdeen in a short while, she seizes the opportunity to say what she hardly trusts herself to do verbally without giving way to her feelings. She wishes to say what a *pang* it is for her to separate from so kind, and dear and valued a friend as Lord Aberdeen has ever been to her since she has known him. The day he became her Prime Minister was a *very happy* one for her.'

During the Garter ceremony, when he took hold of the Queen's hand to raise it to his lips, to his amazement the normally inert little paw came to life and squeezed his hand with a strong and deliberate pressure. He could hardly prevent himself from looking round to see if any of the courtiers had noticed.

And afterwards? The Queen tried Derby, the leader of the Opposition, as was only right and proper, then she tried old Lansdowne, then she tried Clarendon, then she tried Lord John – anyone rather than Palmerston. When they came to see him, Palmerston sat by the fire fanning his face with a newspaper and just hummed and hawed. He knew quite well, as he said himself, that 'I am, for the moment, *l'inévitable*'. The people wanted Pam, guzzling, meddling, irrepressible Pam – dyed whiskers, dubious reputation and all – and Pam is what they got. And George swallowed his chagrin because he knew that 'Palmerston can venture to make a peace, for which the country will thank him, but for which if I had made, they would have talked of cutting my head off'. George went north and watched the trees grow at Haddo. At noon on Saturdays he still sat on the broad flight of steps leading down to the drive and received all who wished to speak to him on local business. He was the last Scottish landlord to keep up this ancient tradition of 'sitting in the gate', a relic of the time when the landlord's justice was the only justice to be had.

And there he sat, looking like a heavyset old minister, with the butler holding the black umbrella over him if it was raining (he was not to be deterred by a soft morning). And if no tenant turned up to complain, he would read a little under the umbrella, Petrarch perhaps (he had returned to his old fondness for the early Italians) or Chateaubriand, or he would chat to Mary or his youngest son Arthur.

One bright morning when the only mist to be seen was on the lake, Mary brought a slender green volume into the little morning-room, that same room where he had eaten his first Aberdeenshire neeps half a century earlier.

'I thought you might care for this, papa.'

'*Tennyson*, oh no, surely you must know my aversion by now. Britons, guard your own, cannon to left of them, cannon to right of them, someone has blundered. Why do you persecute me so?'

'I thought you might be interested to see how Mr Tennyson has returned to his earlier manner. Some of the verses in this book are very beautiful. Come into the garden Maud, for the black bat, night, has flown. He calls it a monodrama.'

'Monomania might be nearer the mark. But to please you, my dear, I shall plough my way through it.'

He took the book with him to the little garden he had made a few miles away in the wild ravines leading down to the sea at Buchan Ness, the most easterly point in Scotland. There, sheltered from the wind and the screech of the gulls, he sat in the rustic summer-house watching the cold green crash of the North Sea waves. And all one grey afternoon he read *Maud*, with that close attention he gave everything – government documents, Athenian ex-voto tablets, poetry and prose in half a dozen languages.

'I hate the dreadful hollow behind the little wood.' From the opening line he was caught – by the command of line and tone, by the melody which no other English poet living, and perhaps none dead, could match, by that lingering, curling way he had of making words stay with you. On and on he read, but as the poem pursued its alluring, erratic course, another feeling rose inside him, got up with a whirr of wings and a screech like a flushed pheasant, a feeling halfway between nausea and alarm. There was something morbid, lascivious even, about the poem. It went too deep and lingered too long in the deep places. And there was a sickening glibness too about the way the poet dragged in war as a purifying force, one which would cleanse society of its money-grubbing callousness and squalor.

When a Mammonite mother kills her babe for a
    burial fee,
And Timour-Mammon grins on a pile of children's
    bones
Is it peace or war? better, war! loud war by land and
    by sea,

War with a thousand battles, and shaking a hundred
  thrones.

But then he would be seduced once again by the
sensuous swing of a lyric:

> A voice by the cedar tree
> In the meadow under the Hall!

And the voice he himself had heard in the woods at
Bentley would come back to him and to regain his
senses he had to shake himself like a terrier.

But regain them he did, and by the time he came to
the closing stanzas his mind was as hard and sharp as
the great granite cliffs around him.

> Let it go or stay, so I wake to the higher aims
> Of a land that has lost for a little her lust of gold
> And love of a peace that was full of wrongs and
>   shames
> And hail once more to the banner of battle unrolled.

Lord Aberdeen removed the plaid rug that was
covering his knees.

> For the long, long canker of peace is over and done,
> And now by the side of the Black and Baltic deep,
> And deathful-grinning mouths of the Fortress,
>   flames
> The blood-red blossom of war with a heart of fire.
> Let it flame or fade, and the war roll down like a
>   wind
> We have proved we have hearts in a cause, we are
>   noble still.

Lord Aberdeen got up and walked along the pink granite pebble path between the wallflowers and forget-me-nots to the end of the terrace which jutted out above the wave-crashed rocks. Leaning on the rustic wooden balustrade with his left hand, he took the green book in his right hand and, pivoting like a discus-thrower of old, hurled it as far as he could into the gathering mist. The light was too dim for his old eyes to see where it landed.

'They have almost finished work on the manse.'

'Have they now?'

'They are waiting for your decision on the church, Father. Is it to be rebuilt?'

'No, I leave that for George.'

'But you have rebuilt all the other churches on the estate. They cannot see why Methlick should be an exception, the present structure is so dilapidated.'

'My church-building days are over. I leave that for the next generation.'

'But, sir –'

'Arthur, the subject is closed, I wish to hear no more of it.'

Mary tried the subject too, bewildered by this refusal. After all, her father-in-law had never shown the slightest confidence in her husband's ability to manage any other project. And the church really did need rebuilding or replacing. Every Sunday, they lumbered along in the huge old coach to be greeted by the minister in his Geneva gown and bands, with the rest of the congregation respectfully assembled out-side the church. Whatever the weather, they would not go in until his lordship had arrived to lead them in. Then they climbed the outside steps to the family loft while down below the minister squeezed past the deaf old women in their red and brown cloaks (who were allowed to sit upon the pulpit stairs so they could hear better), hung up his hat on the minister's peg, and began to read the metrical psalm which was then sung solemnly, unaccompanied, sitting down. And every Sunday, she wondered why HL, as she and Arthur referred to him, refused to notice how ugly and peeling and damp and falling down the place was.

Mary thought he had come to terms with his disappointments. He seemed to worry more about the coughs and fevers of his grandchildren than about public affairs. Melancholy had settled on his old monkey face and was hard to chase off it. But all the time the Subject was there, nagging away at his reason, pricking his pride, stumping him, provoking him.

'You are quite right in supposing that I look back with satisfaction, to the efforts made by me to preserve peace,' he wrote. 'My only cause of regret is that when I found this to be impossible I did not at once retire instead of allowing myself to be dragged into a war which, although strictly justifiable in itself, was most unwise and unnecessary. All this will be acknowledged some day, but the worst of it is that it will require fifty years before men's eyes are opened to the truth.'

After all, a century earlier, Sir Robert Walpole had told them they would soon be wringing their hands over the Spanish War, and posterity adored Sir Robert. Why should not he too be acquitted in about, say, 1919, and carried triumphant from the court of history? But there is no acquittal for scapegoats, the inscriptions are already carved in marble and the revisionists come too late. And besides, our blood was up, was it not? And stayed up.

That much he knew. And the Indian Mutiny confirmed it. 'It seems to me that a warlike and bloodthirsty spirit has been created in the country. The exhortations of our papers in recommending indiscriminate slaughter are abominable, but they are also suicidal, for we could never long exist in India after having taken such means to create the most inveterate spirit of revenge.' It passed belief that *The Times* should nickname the Governor-General 'Clemency' Canning for doing no more than common sense dictated. But then he could scarcely bear to read *The Times* now. On and on it frothed: every mutineer should be executed, every Moslem mosque destroyed, Delhi should be razed and utterly obliterated as a city. 'Every tree and gable end in the place should have its burden in the shape of a mutineer's carcase, but between justice and these wretches steps in a prim philanthropist from Calcutta' – Clemency

Canning the 'Indo-maniac'. Was it worse to belong to the Kremlin School than to be an Indo-maniac, he wondered?

'Oh Delane, Delane,' he murmured.

'Sir?' His son Arthur had not quite caught what he had said.

'I was just reflecting on the world's slow stain.' What had become of the generous young man he had strolled the lobbies with ten years ago?

'Shelley, is it not, father?'

'No, Wordsworth, Arthur.'

'I'm sure it is Shelley.'

'No doubt you are right. My memory has gone.'

Well, that was mostly affectation, but his memory did have a way of drifting back to earlier, and he could not help thinking, lighter brighter days when people talked less about God and less about revenge.

He wandered about the house. After an anxious search, Mary and Arthur would find him standing still in front of the looking-glass in one of the maids' bedrooms, or sitting amongst the logs in the lean-to in the stable yard. Sometimes, looking out of an upper window, they would see his burly bandy-legged figure tottering down the terrace steps and out over the lawn towards the plantations. His gait seemed to have a trancelike quality, as though he were drawn on by some unseen guide. He seemed to have no fixed destination. When he did not return, Arthur would have the pony cart harnessed and trot over the soggy turf and down the great ride (the trees were forty or fifty foot tall now) and find his father leaning on a gate or sitting on a tree stump, staring.

It turned out that his building days were not quite done. One day, Mary found him directing some workmen in the park. They were levering a large stone pedestal into a square hole in the soft earth, then cementing on top of it a storied urn. Inscribed upon the urn she read 'HAUD IMMEMOR'.

'I knew nothing of this, your lordship. May I enquire the significance of the inscription?'

'That is for the learned, my dear.'

She asked Arthur, 'Not unmindful of what, or of whom, do you think?'

'I don't see why you expect me to know. He never speaks to me, never tells me anything I have a right to know. I don't know how much longer I can tolerate these silent meals. The noise of his chewing is becoming intolerable.'

On good days, he would receive distinguished guests, or arbitrate on some Scottish ecclesiastical wrangle, or compose a letter on some fine question of classical archaeology, and he would seem a perfect specimen of a retired statesman. Only on the still evenings of late August, when the thick clouds of midges rose from the lake and the trees seemed to press in against the house, only then could Mary hear the low questioning groans from his room. If only he could recapture his faith (for she would not admit to herself that he had never been much of a believer). He had nothing against transubstantiation, he said, but it was clearly a superstition and it seemed a trifle hard to inflict penalties on a man for believing less than his neighbour in a matter neither of them could comprehend. She tried to have little talks with him, but he insisted on falling asleep.

Then he finally fell asleep in the Lord, more or less. He died at a quarter-to-two in the morning in a high-necked white nightshirt in his high mahogany bed at Argyll House. His son Arthur was holding one of his hands, and his grandson Dod, Mary's son (yet another George) holding the other. Two of his stepsons, Abercorn and Claud Hamilton, were also standing with bowed heads in front of the washstand, and his brother old Admiral John had to flatten himself against the wardrobe as the doctor came to pronounce the verdict which the rest of them could see for themselves. For the old monkey face had turned white and waxy and the sadness had gone from it. The room smelled of camphor and cologne and old man's sweat, and the doctor took the liberty of opening the window on to Argyll Street and let in the noise of the London night.

Years later, Gladstone's mind was still running on Aberdeen. 'He is the man in public life of all others whom I have *loved*. I say emphatically *loved*. I have *loved* others, but never like him.' But George was not at all like Gladstone, and anyway he did not expect to be loved, except by women and children. There was no tortuous, religiose intellectual energy about him. He was a plain man, as Peel had been, and that plainness was gone, that calm plainness that saw things straight and would not colour them with passion, the plainness that had made him seem so odd. In death, he was dubbed the English Aristides, and he would have been flattered and amused by that but at the same time would have shied away from it.

He was buried alongside his two wives in Stanmore church where he had married both of them. Or rather, in the new church they had built at Stanmore next to the old one. The pink ruined walls of the old church were covered with ivy now, and the ivy was covered with snow on that calm, cold, hard, frosty day. Arthur watched the pallbearers – a duke, two earls and Mr Gladstone – walk beside the coffin behind the state coach the Queen had sent with its six horses and postillions and grooms in dress liveries, and he could not stop wondering why his father, who had not worshipped in this parish for years, should have paid for the new church here and should then have refused to rebuild the church at Methlick which he patronised every Sunday and which was in a much worse state.

After the funeral, Arthur went north to Scotland, to the great empty house, a palace now, after all HL's improvements, its walls hung with the finest Italian masters, its demesne a paradise of parterres and lakes and great forests. As he began to clear out HL's drawers, Arthur found that even these were in spotless order, letters all neatly packeted, documents catalogued, clothes threadbare and plain but all tidied away in the appropriate tallboys and armoires.

He was just looking through a drawerful of hunting clothes, breeches and waistcoats, when he saw what looked like a crumpled lavender bag at the back of the drawer. He reached in, and pulled out a scrap of paper rolled like a miniature scroll. There was writing on it. He recognised the jerky script of HL's later years, not always easy to read. But he could make out this inscription right enough:

'And David said to Solomon, My son, as for me, it was in my mind to build an house unto the name of the Lord my God: but the word of the Lord came to me, saying, Thou hast shed blood abundantly, and hast made great wars: thou shalt not build an house unto my name, because thou hast shed much blood upon the earth in my sight (I Chronicles xxii. 7–8).'

For a moment or two, Arthur was nonplussed. HL was more likely to quote Shakespeare or Voltaire than the Scriptures. And then the cloud rolled away, and the mystery of the unbuilt church at Methlick became plain to him. The unbuilding was an expiation, a private expiation, one carried out in the sight of God and not in the sight of Lord Palmerston, but an expiation all the same. And Arthur leant against the cold chestnut wood of the chest of drawers and wept till he felt the salt of the tears at the corner of his mouth.

After lunch, a maid came in and said she did not like to bother him but she had found this in a drawer and thought it might be important. Arthur unrolled another little scroll. The ink was different and the handwriting shakier, suggesting a later date, but the words were the same: And David said to Solomon. As the days went by, other scraps came to light: in HL's desk, in the estate office forestry drawers, in the middle drawer of Mary's dressing-table amidst her artificial flowers and keepsakes. Another was found interleaved in the Cellar Book, and a grubby little blue scrap of paper came to light among the dessert knives. He had secreted them all over the house, perhaps over a period of three or four years. Arthur computed the total number discovered at nineteen but there may well have been more.

Well, I suppose it was a futile little gesture really, a senile obsession, spitting in the wind of history, but still it happened and it seems worth recording.

— VIII —

The bomb fell on a rainy windy night through the cascading plane leaves. It fell with a flat bang on the flat tombstones. It was because they all lay flat, unlike the Christian gravestones, that most of them were already weathered and illegible and now they cracked into a dozen pieces so they were more illegible still. The bomb made a round crater near the wall ten foot deep, with the fragments of tombstone falling into the soft earth like crazy paving. Beyond, in the Mile End Road, there were shouts and cries of pain and soon the first ringing of fire engines. But here in the cemetery there was only the sound of the tomb shards scraping against each other and settling into the earth. And the ghosts made no noise as they rose from the gaping graves, not even the ghost in row one, grave 26,

David Pacifico (birth date illegible, died 12 April 1854).

He rose with some reluctance, he had been happy there behind the Mile End Road, amongst the Mocattas and the Montefiores, the Pereiras and the Bensusans. It was a good billet, as they said down Whitechapel way, a place where a man could rest easy after all the troubles of that mortal life. And he had had troubles – cheated and persecuted by half-a-dozen governments, hustled from one place to the next, house burnt down by the ignorant mob – why had they blamed him and not Baron Rothschild for that abominable Judas business being cancelled? Three times, no, four, he had set himself up as a decent respectable merchant, and every time he had been bullied and cozened and duped and diddled until he was just a small-time moneylender lending tin he hadn't got to people who couldn't afford to pay him the interest. Even so, in his last three years, half the traders in Petticoat Lane swore by him, would have gone out of business if it wasn't for old Passy, but still it was a poor way to end up. If the cards had fallen right, he could have been a Rothschild and had processions cancelled out of respect for *his* feelings. Well, it all came to the same in the end, old Nathan Rothschild might have had a procession a mile long when they carried his carcase down the Mile End Road but he finished up in the same borough as *le chevalier* Pacifico – they were practically rubbing shoulders in death, you might say. And say what you like about the English, they knew the difference between right and wrong, and they knew you had to stand up for a man's rights whoever or wherever he was, D. Pacifico included. Many a time, he had lulled himself to sleep with the last words of that speech, the *civis romanus sum* one (there's David mumbling that precious civil service speech again, as his dear wife would say). But still, when all was said and done, it was the greatest speech ever delivered in the House of Commons, everyone agreed on that, and it was all about him, D. Pacifico, and when he walked down Bury Street, St. Mary Axe, the City gentlemen would whisper to the ladies who he was and the ladies would look at him in a way they had not looked at him since he was a young consul. He owed all this to Lord Palmerston, of course, but he owed it to his fellow Britons even more. They were the ones who had cheered for him and for Pam as Prime Minister. Pacifico and Palmerston, they went together as snugly as beer and skittles. A Jew could be as good an Englishman as a Welshie or a Scot, a Jew could be an MP, could be Prime Minister yet. Of course, there was prejudice still, any fool could see that. He didn't care for *Oliver Twist*, for example, he read it the first summer he came to England and he thought Fagin was a vile caricature, and he threw the book out of the window of the train to Margate when he was taking the family for a day by the seaside, which the book had utterly ruined.

But still, there was prejudice everywhere in the world if you went looking for it. The Englishmen he didn't care for weren't the ones who couldn't abide foreigners, Jews especially. The ones he didn't like were the snivelly weasel-worded Englishmen who wouldn't stick up for you when you were in a bit of trouble, the ones who prated about peace and diplomacy when they should have been going full steam ahead with guns ablazing – that Lord Aberdeen, for example, he was a stuck up lump of dreck if ever there was one. And that Lord Derby, he was worse. How he had gone on about their mahogany double bed, as though he and Mrs P. had no right to a decent place to sleep and his daughter Rachel had no right to silk stockings because she was the daughter of a petty usurer. Snobs, that's what they were, when you came down to it, snobs who hadn't a clue about the real world. Why hadn't Monsieur Pacifico tried the courts? Had Milord Aberdeen ever been in a Greek court, he'd know why not. If ever he got a chance, he would haunt Lord Aberdeen, haunt him rotten until he realised what it was like to be a man of business without money or friends or influence, trying to keep afloat.

Then as the bomb smoke drifted away into the wet night, the ghost of Don Pacifico realised that in fact this *was* his chance. And so he rose out of his shattered tomb with a gentle sucking noise like the noise of a long cork being drawn from an old bottle or, to be honest, more like the noise of an old woman farting, but as only he could hear it who cared? And his spirit swung easily through the branches of the shattered plane tree and up and out into the night sky, above the shouting and the firebells and all the grief and pain. The sky was still lit by huge explosions, great orange-yellow flashes so that he could see in one sweeping gaze all those churches that reared their startling spires and turrets out of the Stepney squalor – St. Georges-in-the-East, St. Anne's Limehouse and the huge thrusting rocket of Christ Church, Spital-fields. He floated without effort above them all, at a lazy rate, the speed of thistledown or a planing pigeon.

He knew where he was going. He had made his preliminary reconnaissance. Many a time when his wife thought he had gone to see a client, he had taken an omnibus up west and gone to stand outside Derby House or Argyll House (handy that his persecutors should live virtually next door to one another) and waited for Lord Derby or Lord Aberdeen to return from Parliament or from a ride in the Park. He would stand unnoticed in the knot of idlers outside the lodge gates and watch the footman open the carriage door for his lordship and see the carriage bounce as the bulky old gent placed his foot on the little step. More often, Lord Aberdeen would walk home, he was a great walker, and Don Pacifico had the pleasure – yes, it was a pleasure – of bumping up against the burly old gentleman as he rounded the Regent Street corner with that odd clumsy walk of his, like a man shifting a sack of coal from one shoulder to the other. Why did Don Pacifico condescend to rub shoulders with his persecutors, what was the pleasure in it? He couldn't say exactly, he just liked to keep them under observation. With Lord Aberdeen in particular, it was a positive delight to dog that proud old bumbler. The summer two years before he, well, dropped out of things and went to Mile End, Don Pacifico had received a dogcart in payment for a bad debt, with a broken-down old bay horse attached, one step up from a rag-and-bone man's equipage, but he liked to take the air in it and trot round London following his lordship when *he* was taking the air. One summer afternoon he followed him down to Greenwich with the nag blowing like a hurricane. Then the next Sunday he followed him all the way up to Stanmore. Whew, that was a haul and a half. He thought the nag would never get up the hill. When his lordship went into the church to pay his respects to his two wives, two for the price of one in a manner of speaking, the nag munched the grass in the graveyard till there wasn't a blade left between the gravestones. Then he followed him up through the trees along the lake to pay a call on his stepson Lord Abercorn and to see the old Priory where he had lived when he was first married and which he liked better than anywhere in the world, according to the old gardener who Don Pacifico had chummed up with while the horse was grazing on the verge. It was a beautiful place, the Priory, surrounded by a lovely park, no danger of the mob breaking in there and burning your furniture and terrifying your wife and daughter to death, a real place of safety, not a place for the likes of Pacifico.

He planed on, letting himself drift in a northerly direction – how agreeable it was this weightless silent motion, skimming over fresh snow on a sledge was the nearest thing to it he could imagine. There was Piccadilly Circus, he could tell by the pattern of the streets, not by the lights because when the bombs stopped the whole city was dark. At first he had scarcely noticed this because the flashes of the explosions were so bright and frequent, but now the explosions had utterly ceased and there was not a glimmer of light to be seen below him. All the same, he knew his West End and managed to identify the curve of Regent Street and the turning three-quarters of the way up it, just before you got to Mr Nash's round church at the top.

But where was the wall with the rusticated pillars, where were the iron railings and the high gates? Where was the pediment and the plain façade with the fat old porter waddling out of his box to undo the gates? Gone, all gone. And in their place, hey what was this? A big ornate flashy sort of building with pillars and cherubs and advertising hoardings all over it. Parl – Pal – Palladium, what a fancy name for such a vulgar common sort of place. He floated down and roosted on the glass roof of its little dome, but he could see nothing since every pane of glass was blacked out from the inside, but he could hear something, a distant voice that seemed to be singing in a drowsy sort of way.

The ghost of Don Pacifico fluttered over the jumble of roofs at the back of the building and found a ventilation grille like a funnel on a ship. Not without apprehension, he slid down the shaft of it for what seemed like miles, then he came round a bend and the shaft began to glow with light. Another bend, and the light was as bright as day. Peering down, he found that he was hovering above a huge stage flooded with a light brighter than he had ever seen in his life.

And on the stage there was the most peculiar act: five elderly gents, rather moth-eaten and broken down mostly, all wearing that new sort of billycock hat – what was it called? a bowler, that was it – and flashy suits like you might wear to the races and in the middle of them another elderly party wearing a ragged old rabbitskin coat like the poorest traders in Petticoat Lane wore in the winter. It was the rabbitskin party who was doing the singing in a sleepy wailing voice while the other old gents kept time and pretended to dance and fell over each other and made silly faces and the audience, which he couldn't see from his perch but must be enormous, was laughing itself silly and rocking the rafters.

What was he singing now?

'Who do you think you are kidding Mr Hiddler
When you say you've got old England on the run.'

He knew the type of song: patriotic, a street ballad,
you could buy it for a penny on the corner. Catchy
tune. You couldn't beat a good ballad. A country
marched on its ballads. This Hiddler had better watch
out. But what had become of Argyll House? Had he
been away so long? As he framed the question, it
seemed a slippery sort of speculation. What was 'long'
exactly? A long time, that was the phrase but he wasn't
quite sure what it meant. The elderly gents skipped
towards the front of the stage, held hands like
schoolgirls and bowed. One of them curtsied and the
one next to him knocked his bowler hat off. Then the
rabbitskin party began to sing again in his sweet
ambling old man's voice. It was an odd little song
about an umbrella mender, a singing umbrella mender
by the sound of it because he warbled toodle luma
luma toddle-ay as he fixed your brolly with his
thingumajig, or when business was slack sharpened
knives for all the wives in the neighbourhood. He
could mend a clock too, or a broken heart apparently.
Don Pacifico well remembered the umbrella man who
had his pitch just behind the Bank of England, a dark
little fellow sitting cross-legged on the pavement with
his old iron clamp between his knees straightening the
spokes and stretchers of brollies which had been
blown inside out by the wind. Any umbrellas to mend

today. Don Pacifico found himself singing along. He was really beginning to enjoy the show, but he knew he had work to do. Another night such as this might not come again.

So on he floated back up the ventilation shaft and out into the air again and then up over the Prince Regent's Park and across the canal to pick up the long straight arrow of the Edgware Road, the old Watling Street, which would take him almost the whole way up to Stanmore. From the air the darkened streets seemed cold and friendless now. He lay on his back and experimented with floating as a swimmer floats. The sky above him seemed empty at first, then out of the corner of his eye far above him he saw mysterious slender objects like giant geese. They were flying away from him, in formation like geese too, down towards Kent and the Channel, he supposed. And they droned, these dark geese, a relentless snoring noise, incessant, unvarying. On and away they flew, until the sky was empty again, and even the snoring grew fainter and fainter until he could hear nothing except the whisper of the breeze.

He knew where to find the Priory too, in the trees at the top of the hill just above the lake. He alighted silently on the footpath that led up through the low woods of birch and hazel and looked for the little turning to the left that would bring him up to the house. To his surprise, he immediately tripped and found himself falling into a deep muddy trench with sodden leaves at the bottom. Picking himself up and trying to clamber up the other side, he immediately ran into a high wire fence. The wire had strange little spikes all the way along it, like reinforced teazles. He edged along the fence hoping to find a gate or a break, but the fence seemed to run all the way down the hill. Ten foot high at least it must be, with another roll of this horrible wire-teazle stuff running along the top of it. Ah, there was a signpost flapping on the wire. Peering in the darkness, Don Pacifico could only just make out the wording on the notice: 'This is a prohibited place within the meaning of the Official Secrets Act. Unauthorised persons entering the area may be arrested and prosecuted.'

Well, they could not prohibit *him*. His situation might have its disadvantages, but one thing was sure, no peeler was going to put the bracelets on him. He was immune, invulnerable to all their arresting and prosecuting. All he had to do was to hop over this contemptible fence and he could stroll and take his ease in his lordship's grounds as long as he fancied.

He made the little kneesbend and hop which he had discovered was the way to take off – and was annoyed to find that his ascent was no longer quite so effortless. His legs, which had seemed as tireless as a kangaroo's, seemed to have lost something of their spring. He cleared the fence all right, but he found it a relief to come down to land again on the other side and walk up to the house like any ordinary mortal.

When he climbed the steps to the terrace, he found that he needed to pause to get his breath back. Then he noticed that the rooms on the ground floor were all shuttered and dark and it was only the lights on the first floor that were burning bright, so he would need to roost again. Kneesbend, hop – he only just made it this time and found himself trembling on a narrow ledge or cornice, clinging to a balustrade. A decidedly humiliating position: ghosts were supposed to make other people tremble, not teeter with knees turned to jelly on some damned balcony.

He soon forgot his resentment. Thick black material covered the length of the long windows, but the windows had been opened a little to let the air in, and the material flapped in the night breeze, so that now and then he could see round the edge of it and into the long brightly lit room. It was barely furnished and without decoration on the walls except for a huge map with some sort of counters or little flags in different colours stuck to it. Two young women in sky-blue costume were moving the flags around. One of them had strange little muffs clamped to her ears by an iron hoop over her head. A man also dressed in sky blue was pointing to various positions on the map with what looked like a billiard cue. His eyes were blue too, an even more brilliant blue than his costume, and he had grand moustachios like an Albanian brigand. It was peculiar, this costume, severely cut with baffling little flaps and pockets. He supposed it must be a military uniform, but it was so austere he was half inclined to put it down as the habit of some eccentric religious brotherhood. After all, the women were dressed in the same material, yet they could scarcely be members of the same regiment (but their skirts were much too short for a nunnery). He watched entranced as this azure sect went about their tasks. Beneath their brisk and businesslike concentration on matters in hand, they were clearly in a state of high excitement. They were exalted. He hadn't seen people so thrilled since there had been a run on 'Change, the first year he came to London, and he had watched from the gallery as the brokers and jobbers rushed about the floor to cover their positions, except that they shouted and flapped their hands, and the sky blues didn't flap. They did the necessary, as he would say, without fuss.

Don Pacifico stretched forward, craning his neck as close as he could to the gap between the long windows.

'Two more safely landed at Biggin Hill, sir.'

'No further casualties reported from Manton.'

How English they were, those voices. How clipped and swallowed. In general he preferred Italian, but there was something about the voice of an English-woman.

'Well, it looks as if jerry's calling it a night. It has been a long night, ladies and gentlemen, and a hard one, but I think we can say we have seen it through. Daphne, could you get me Air Marshal Leigh-Mallory.'

'Yes sir.'

Yes sir, how wonderful it would be to have an Englishwoman with blonde hair and a blue shirt saying yessir. And Air Marshal yet – what sort of a title was that. He had heard of Celestial Emperors, but an Air Marshal, in England – there was madness abroad. Who were all these people in these peculiar costumes, Lord Aberdeen's servants, or Lord Abercorn's? Where were their lordships, and their ladies? How and why had this ancient seat been taken over by these alien beings?

His brain grew fuzzy and dim. He felt his grip on the balustrade weakening. In his legs he had scarcely any feeling at all. Some obscure intimation came to him, some message attempting to get through, indecipherable but inescapable too. Now the feeling had gone in his hands also, he could no longer feel the cold wet iron of the railings. What was the message? Something was up. The game was up? No, not that. His, his, what was it, his time, yes his time was up. Time, the word seemed to have no meaning, it was only an empty ring in his ears, but then his hearing was fading too. Everything was going, going, ladies and gentlemen (oh he had been an auctioneer once in Smyrna, or was it in Aleppo), going, going – and silently, with only a whisper like the whisper of a hot-iron gliding over silk, the ghost of Don Pacifico was gone, a pale white skein in the windy night, at best a memory and not a happy one.

— NOTES —

I

George Gordon was born in 1784. At the age of seven, he succeeded his father as Lord Haddo.

His distant cousin, George Gordon Byron, was born in 1788, and succeeded his great-uncle as the sixth Lord Byron in 1798.

From 1795 to 1800, Haddo went to Harrow School. Harry 'Cupid' Temple was his exact contemporary. Byron arrived at school the year after he had left. So did Sir Robert Peel. Byron and Peel became great friends in Drury's House. Temple and Haddo did not.

On the death of his grandfather in 1801, Haddo became the fourth Earl of Aberdeen.

II

After the Peace of Amiens was signed in March 1802, British citizens were free to travel to the Continent again and to make the Grand Tour, for the first time since the French war began in 1793.

While in Athens, Aberdeen made friends with Giovanni Battista Lusieri, Lord Elgin's agent (Elgin was at this time a prisoner of war in France, having been trapped there when the Peace of Amiens broke down). It is suggested that Aberdeen may have been one of 'two very rich English gentlemen' who were prepared to offer fifty thousand piastres (four hundred pounds) for the frieze from the Parthenon. As it is, the British Museum contains a dozen sculptures which he brought back, most notably the 'Aberdeen Head' from Messene.

Byron's attacks on 'Athenian Aberdeen' began in *English Bards and Scottish Reviewers* (1809), and continued in *Childe Harold's Pilgrimage* (1812).

III

Lady Hester Stanhope kept house for her uncle, Pitt the Younger, at Bowling Green House, Putney, from 1803 until his death in 1806. After living in Wales for a time, she left England for the Levant and never saw her native land again.

Sir Walter Scott described Bentley Priory as 'the resort of the most distinguished part of the fashionable world'. He himself, the Prince Regent, Sir Thomas Lawrence, Kemble the actor and Richard Brinsley Sheridan were among regular visitors to the eighteenth-century villa, which was enlarged by Sir John Soane for Lord Abercorn.

Aberdeen and Catherine were married in July 1805. Jane was born in 1807, Caroline in 1808, and Alice in 1809. Catherine died on 24 February 1812.

Harry Temple had succeeded his father and become the third Lord Palmerston in 1802, but being an Irish peer had no seat in the Lords and was entitled to stand for election to the Commons, which he first did, unsuccessfully, at a by-election in 1806 for the Cambridge University seat left vacant by the death of Pitt. In November that year, he stood again in the General Election, for Horsham. Again he failed, but by challenging the verdict, he compelled the bailiffs to take the proper course of declaring all four candidates elected, leaving it to Parliament to decide which to unseat. Palmerston was unseated. He finally became an MP when he was returned unopposed for Newport the following year.

Aberdeen set out for the Continent on 10 August 1813. He was left a wide discretion to negotiate, so long as the peace confined France 'within her natural borders' and provided adequately for the tranquillity and independence of Europe.

As well as passing through Terezin (Theresienstadt), Aberdeen would also have passed through Lidice, Dresden, Breslau and many other places which were to resound in the history of our own times.

Wagner wrote to his father: 'Oh this town of Teplice with its endless vistas; it is really the most beautiful place I know.' Goethe and Beethoven met here in 1812, a year before the two Emperors and the king of Prussia met to sign their treaty of Alliance against Napoleon. Teplice is now a filthy decaying industrial town which stinks of brown coal.

British officers frequently carried umbrellas on the battlefield.

Even the Duke of Wellington took one with him, although he did not approve of their use during the enemy's fire. Marshal Soult was startled by the resolution displayed by *les efféminés avec leurs parapluies*. During the Waterloo campaign, A. M. de Montebel recorded: 'the enemy hussars advanced rapidly towards our cavalry. It was raining, and the English officers were on horseback, each with an umbrella in hand, which seemed to me eminently ridiculous. All at once the English closed their umbrellas, hung them on their saddles, drew their sabres and threw themselves upon our chasseurs who defended themselves bravely; but their mounts lacked the vigour of the horses of their adversaries.'

Abercorn's heir, Viscount Hamilton, died on 27 May 1814. His widow Harriet married Aberdeen on 8 July 1815, and had four more sons, George, Alexander, Douglas and Arthur, and a daughter, Frances. Arthur became Lord Stanmore and wrote the first life of his father (1893). No male outside his family has ever written about Aberdeen. The official biography, by Lady Frances Balfour (2 vols. 1922), is a miserable botch. Two more recent lives of Aberdeen by Lucille Iremonger (1978) and Muriel Chamberlain (1983) have made an excellent start on restoring him to life. The present author is deeply indebted to both and to Stanmore's *The Earl of Aberdeen*. Lord Abercorn died in 1818 leaving Aberdeen to administer his estates in Scotland and Ireland. He also left him large sums of money. The grateful Aberdeen thought of quartering the Abercorn coat of arms with his own to symbolise the union of the two families. Instead, he hyphenated their surnames to become George Hamilton-Gordon.

The only work Aberdeen himself ever published was *An Inquiry into the Principles of Beauty and Grecian Architecture with an Historical View of the Rise and Progress of the Art in Greece* (1822).

Arthur privately printed, but did not publish, his father's correspondence in nine volumes. Gladstone imposed a veto on publication, fearing embarrassing disclosures, but in any case there would probably have been little demand for the papers of the scapegoat of the Crimea. Aberdeen's correspondence with Princess Lieven was published in two volumes by the Camden Society (1938–39), ed. E. Jones-Parry. By then she was more famous than he.

VI

David Pacifico was born in Gibraltar in the same year as Aberdeen and Palmerston, 1784. He moved to Portugal, where his property was confiscated by Don Miguel because he had supported the liberals. In 1835, he became Portuguese consul-general in Morocco, and in 1837 in Greece, but the complaints against him were so numerous that he was dismissed from the service in 1842. He settled in Athens, living as a merchant. His house was burnt down at Easter, 1847. He eventually received a hundred and twenty thousand drachmas for the plunder of his house, and five hundred pounds as compensation for his sufferings.

He finally settled in London and died at 15 Bury Street, St. Mary Axe on 12 April 1854, and was buried in the Spanish burial ground, Mile End, two days later.

VII

Aberdeen kissed hands as Prime Minister at Osborne on 19 December 1852, and resigned on 30 January 1855. War was declared on 28 March 1854. Sebastopol was finally captured on 9 September 1855, although peace came about less from military success than as a result of the international negotiations which had continued throughout the fighting. The Treaty of Paris signed in March 1856 was based on the Four Points of which Aberdeen had approved and believed he had come close to securing in December 1854.

Palmerston was Prime Minister from February 1855 to February 1858, and again from June 1859 until his death in October 1865.

Maud was published in the summer of 1855. By October, eight thousand copies had been sold, but the reception of the poem was not entirely favourable. *Tait's Edinburgh Magazine* said in September: 'If any man comes forward to say or sing that the slaughter of 30,000 Englishmen in the Crimea tends to prevent women poisoning their babies, for the sake of the burial fees, in Birmingham, he is bound to show cause, and not bewilder our notions of morals and of lexicography by calling thirty years of intermitted war . . . a "long long *canker* of peace".' For the second edition the following year, Tennyson changed the phrase to 'the peace that I deemed no peace'.

VIII

The Spanish and Portuguese Jews' Cemetery was bombed by the Luftwaffe on 23 September 1940. Part of it still stands in the grounds of Queen Mary and Westfield College, Mile End Road.

Argyll House had been demolished after Aberdeen's death. The Palladium Theatre, an exuberant work of the great theatre architect Frank Matcham, opened on the site in 1910.

Bentley Priory had become the headquarters of RAF Fighter Command in 1936. The Battle of Britain was directed from the house by Air Chief Marshal Dowding, later Lord Dowding of Bentley Priory. It is today the headquarters of RAF No. 11 Group, which provides the air defence for much of eastern Britain, including Aberdeenshire and Tennyson's wolds.

JOHN BANVILLE

The Book of Evidence

'I have read books that are as cleverly constructed as this one and I can think of a few – but not many – writers who can match Banville's technical brilliance, but I have read no other novel that illustrates so perfectly a single epiphany. It is, in its cold, terrifying way, a masterpiece'
Maureen Freely, *Literary Review*

'Compelling and brutally funny from a master of his craft'
Patrick Gale, *Daily Telegraph*

'Banville must be fed up being told how beautifully he writes, but on this occasion he has excelled himself in a flawlessly flowing prose whose lyricism, patrician irony and aching sense of loss are reminiscent of *Lolita*'
Observer

'Completely compelling reading . . . not only entertains but informs, startles and disturbs'
Irish Independent

J. M. COETZEE

The Master of Petersburg

'Anyone interested in the power of fiction to move us and
extend our sense of life should get hold of this book'
Spectator

'A harsh, eloquent critique of the human condition. It is
also a subtle, powerful, superbly written personal
testament. The bleakness of the vision is tempered only
by the certainty that life can be material for art. This is art.
The case is proven'
Sunday Times

'An intense and deep book'
Guardian

'A *tour de force* . . . Utterly engrossing, this is a book
to cherish'
Marie Claire

A Selected List of Fiction Available from Minerva

While every effort is made to keep prices low, it is sometimes necessary to increase prices at short notice. Mandarin Paperbacks reserves the right to show new retail prices on covers which may differ from those previously advertised in the text or elsewhere.

The prices shown below were correct at the time of going to press.

☐	7493 9044 1	**The Book of Evidence**	John Banville	£5.99
☐	7493 9962 7	**Senor Vivo and the Coca Lord**	Louis de Bernières	£5.99
☐	7493 9857 4	**The Troublesome Offspring of Cardinal Guzman**		
			Louis de Bernières	£6.99
☐	7493 9130 8	**The War of Don Emmanuel's Nether Parts**	Louis de Bernières	£4.99
☐	7493 9816 7	**Alma Cogan**	Gordon Burn	£5.99
☐	7493 9632 6	**The Master of Petersburg**	J. M. Coetzee	£5.99
☐	7493 9960 0	**Trick or Treat**	Lesley Glaister	£4.99
☐	7493 9883 3	**How late it was, how late**	James Kelman	£6.99
☐	7493 9112 X	**Hopeful Monsters**	Nicholas Mosley	£7.99
☐	7493 9618 0	**Shear**	Tim Parks	£5.99
☐	7493 9704 7	**Ulverton**	Adam Thorpe	£5.99
☐	7493 9747 0	**Swing Hammer Swing!**	Jeff Torrington	£5.99
☐	7493 9134 0	**Rebuilding Coventry**	Sue Townsend	£5.99

All these books are available at your bookshop or newsagent, or can be ordered direct from the address below. Just tick the titles you want and fill in the form below.

Cash Sales Department, PO Box 5, Rushden, Northants NN10 6YX.
Phone: 01933 414000 : Fax: 01933 414047.

Please send cheque, payable to 'Reed Book Services Ltd.', or postal order for purchase price quoted and allow the following for postage and packing:

£1.00 for the first book, 50p for the second; **FREE POSTAGE AND PACKING FOR THREE BOOKS OR MORE PER ORDER.**

NAME (Block letters) ....

ADDRESS ....

....

☐ I enclose my remittance for ....

☐ I wish to pay by Access/Visa Card Number ☐☐☐☐☐☐☐☐☐☐☐☐☐☐☐☐

Expiry Date ☐☐☐☐

Signature ....

Please quote our reference: MAND